THE TROUBLE WiTH MURDER...
AT THE
HALL

THE TROUBLE WITH MURDER...
AT THE
HALL

ANDREA NELSON

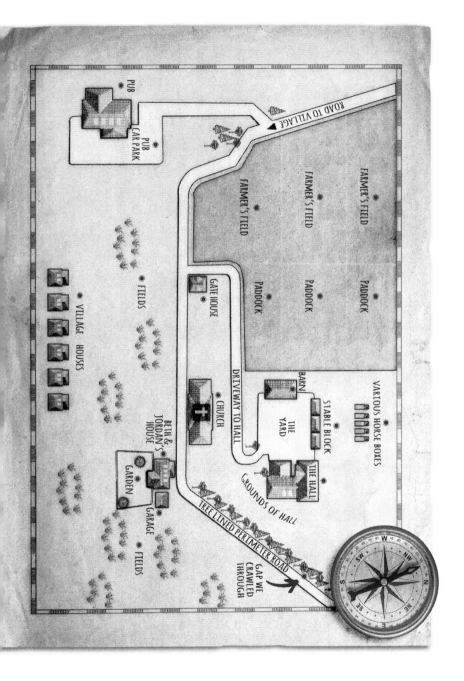

CONTENTS

Chapter One   9

Chapter Two   21

Chapter Three   33

Chapter Four   37

Chapter Five   45

Chapter Six   53

Chapter Seven   65

Chapter Eight   77

Chapter Nine   85

Chapter Ten   95

Chapter Eleven   111

Chapter Twelve   129

Chapter Thirteen   137

Chapter Fourteen   149

Chapter Fifteen   157

Chapter Sixteen   167

Who's Who   175

CHAPTER ONE

"Monty!"

"You're through to the voicemail of Monty Peebles. Don't leave a message, Beth, go away! Goodbye."

"Monty, don't be an arse! Did you get the notification about the ghost walk?"

Beth was hopeful that ignoring Monty's initial resistance would open the door to changing the direction of the conversation.

Beth is an avid ghost hunter. Her life has been consumed by stories of mystery and theories about what happens to you when you die. Beth longs to see a ghost. Having been on many ghost hunts but never having seen a single thing, she could be forgiven for 'giving up the ghost' and diverting her attention to something more ordinary, but that was never going to happen. On the one hand, such is her love for her night-time adventures, with such an imagination, that she was able to convince herself and Monty that some ghoul or other was following them.

Monty's life, on the other hand had, at no point, been consumed by any such intrigue. He loved his life. He enjoyed his lunches with fine wine and great food. He loved clean clothes and well tailored jackets, trousers and hats. His happy places were the many fine diners in and around the Knightsbridge area. This pest called Beth had almost died on him when they first met and has been a pain ever since. Except he didn't mean that, he loved Beth and her zest for life. In truth, she had provided him with the most fun he'd ever imagined having during the past 15 years. He did, however, feel the need to curb her enthusiasm from time to time.

Conversations like the one they were about to have had always started and ended in the same way; his refusal to join in, her total lack of acceptance of that refusal, his agreement to join her and then their mutual excitement about the whole thing.

Today, however, Monty did have reason to say he couldn't go.

"Yes, Beth, I *did* get the notification. I have also been notified this morning at some ridiculous time that Auntie Mildred is en route from South Africa and has requested that I pick her up from Heathrow this afternoon, so time is not on my side."

"What luck – I'm picking Jordan up from the airport today; we could go together."

This news was well received by Monty who, for as much as he says you can't spend enough on good wine, did not feel the same way about his cars. He was currently driving a 16-year-old Golf – the gears crunched, the bodywork was appalling, the interior was full of all sorts of crap, including newspapers (Monty collected them). As a journalist, he would pick holes in the articles of other journalists and make notes within the paper about their written work. He was very critical of the tabloids – less so about the broadsheets whose work was (in his opinion) well researched and generally better informed. He also had notepads everywhere. He made notes about everything, but had so many pads he couldn't ever find those very important notes when he needed them.

Beth currently drives a brand new Range Rover. It was clean both inside and out. This was nothing to do with Beth and everything to do with Jordan who, by his own admission, had Car Cleanliness OCD. Once, in an impatient moment, Beth couldn't wait for the air con to clear the windscreen, so she wiped it with her hand. Jordan, in complete disbelief, had to go indoors for the glass cleaner and relevant cloth (you simply can't use any old cloth for that smear-free finish).

"OK, let's do that then, but we will never make the walk no matter how hard you try to fit it in." Monty, now happy that he could travel in comfort and warmth – in a clean smelling car that his aunt would certainly approve of.

Once they had worked out the timings of the airport pick-ups, allowing time for the drive home and the inevitable M25 crawl between certain junctions, Beth concluded that they could just do it.

"What you have failed to notice, Monty, is that the Hall is only two minutes from our house, well, just under a mile."

"Indeed it is, but what do I do with Auntie Mildred?"

"We can drop Jordan home, he can sit with Auntie Mildred until we are done and then I can drive you both home."

"I love the way you just assume Jordan will be OK with that – he's never even met her."

"I know; that's why I'm assuming he'll be OK with it."

Auntie Mildred was a complete diamond. At 88 you'd think she would be ready for a lifetime of sitting down with a cup of tea watching the same rubbish on TV every day. Not so. In fact, this tour de force was a moped driving mad thing who was, in truth, a danger to anyone she shared a road with. Monty was fairly certain that her prolonged absences in South Africa diverted the authorities' attentions away from her by way of re-examination of both her eyesight and ability to drive lawfully and legally.

Auntie Mildred didn't care for rules – she certainly didn't obey any of them. In South Africa it seemed (from the stories she'd told) that no-one else cared for rules either, so her dreadful attention to road safety went unnoticed. Auntie Mildred was also a people hater. Everyone she met she would treat with complete disdain.

Jordan and Beth had married almost 10 years ago. Initially, he had been an investor and had helped to build up the profiles and profits of a variety of companies.

Nowadays, Jordan was the main shareholder in a silver mine in Australia (Northern Territory, to be exact). He didn't spend as much time over there as he probably should, but he had a very good team and his attention to detail and management ran through the veins of his management team. He and Beth met when they were both in Harrods – Beth was buying a bra and the strap caught onto Jordan's belt. Once they had stopped laughing, they went for coffee and have pretty much been together ever since.

At their time of meeting, Beth had worked for a bank. It had been a job she hated – the uniform was dreadful and the customers were rude. On one occasion, she had asked a lady when her baby was due; she was in fact just very rotund. This was brought up in her annual assessment and, as a result, was only awarded a 3% pay rise rather than the 4.5% awarded to the other cashiers. That earmarked the end of that particular career.

As soon as they were married, Jordan felt that Beth should leave the bank and take some time out to decide what she really wanted to do next and not to feel she needed to rush into anything.

It's fair to say that he hadn't imagined that 10 years on she would still be working that one out.

They loved each other unconditionally. Jordan had even been out with the two Ghostly Go-Getters on a few occasions – secretly, he enjoyed the whole thing – it was fun and a bit scary at the same time. He loved Monty as much as Beth did. He enjoyed the fireside stories of his family and childhood. Both Beth and Jordan had relatively quiet families and upbringings. Beth had been brought up on a farm so spent most of her time climbing trees and fishing for newts as a young girl with her best friend, Trish (who was now a senior member of the clinical development team for a company who worked with the Government). In her teens, Beth loved nothing more than racing around on ponies, bikes and trailers with the boys in the village, but by the time she reached 14, she found make-up and fashion, then all of that changed. Everyone knew though that Beth was as sharp as a razor, didn't miss a trick, would help anyone and was quite fearless. Most people who knew her loved Beth. The ones who didn't clearly didn't know her, as her mother would say. Her family was solid and she had a great relationship with her parents and her sister.

Jordan had always been a complete risk taker. He had never worked for anyone but himself. He was of the opinion that if you didn't own it, you didn't respect it, so by working for himself he only had himself to blame if anything went wrong. The investment in the silver mine was not something he thought would or could last as long as it had done, but he was financially grateful for the lifestyle this had allowed them both to have. Beth was equally grateful for that and her husband's drive and determination.

Jordan's family were disjointed. His parents were divorced and his relationship with them evaporated at the same time. His sister was odd. They loved each other but she was a solicitor and treated him like a client; he was an entrepreneur but treated her like a sister that he loved. He decided in his 20s that he would probably always be a client to his sister, but remained hopeful this would change one day.

As she entered the M25 from the M11, Monty felt the need to ask Beth a few simple Highway Code questions – ones he felt she should know.

"Turn the radio up, Monty, and focus on something else. I have never had points for speeding."

"I would suggest you are very lucky in that case, but please slow down, Beth, I keep bringing up the same bite of my sandwich."

"What reason should we give Auntie Mildred for the diversion? I was thinking we could say that you've been asked to write an article about the owner of the Hall, so I am going along as the introduction."

"I don't think she will care either way, so long as she is fed and watered and. in fact, Jordan is the perfect host – he won't want to talk to her as much as she won't want to listen."

The traffic was slow at best which infuriated Beth – they wouldn't be late but she had wanted to find a double space to park – she was absolutely crap at parking and, judging by the state of Monty's car, he was just as bad.

Once parked, they made their way to arrivals to wait for Jordan. Beth knew that he would take slightly longer than anyone else – he knew she secretly liked to get a bottle of perfume from duty-free and he usually forgot at departure, so he made the purchase on arrival.

"Hey, sexy!" shouted Beth as she saw Jordan emerge through the doors. The chap in front of her looked round and smiled – surely he knew she wasn't talking to him, he had hairs sprouting from his ears and in full view – the same degree of growth was emerging from each nostril. Ugh!

The joy on Jordan's face was clear for all to see. Beth ran and jumped up to him.

"You smell lovely," she said to him – he always did, especially when he'd bought her perfume. He'd try on all the aftershave but could never remember which one he really liked, so he didn't buy anything for himself. His was more of a fusion of fragrance never to be recreated.

"You look fab, Beth, I missed you. Can't wait for a nice relaxing bath, a glass of wine that doesn't burn the back of my throat and a lovely sleep in our own bed. Hey, isn't that Monty over there? Monty!"

"You look like death, Jordan – your eyes are resting on your shoes – in fact, what the bloody hell are they on your feet? I bet the last thing you want is to entertain my aunt tonight."

Jordan had forgotten to remove his in-flight slippers. They were his own slippers his mother had bought for him one year. He hated the design, but had to surrender to their comfort during his long flights.

"Hang on," said Jordan, stopping dead in his tracks, "what did you just say about your aunt? And Beth, why do I think this has something to do with you?"

All was explained.

Whilst Jordan was not best pleased, he didn't complain just as his wife had never complained when he needed to jump on a plane within a moment's notice, always taking him to and from various airports.

They waited for Auntie Mildred.

Almost all passengers had arrived and already left the airport to the point when Monty thought he should question whether she had boarded the flight. Then, they heard a noise. Monty knew who was responsible for the noise, but the other two were yet to get a visual of the terror that was Auntie Mildred.

"Get your filthy, grubby hands off me! I am more than capable of walking in a straight line and certainly more capable of standing upright than that poor sod over there."

Everyone looked at "the poor sod", which turned out to be an old lady who was bent double.

Auntie Mildred, both Beth and Jordan observed, was certainly not representative of a typical 88-yearold. She wasn't tall, but held herself very well indeed and had a very young appearance, both in style and demeanour.

They were about to find out, however, that this lady of aristocratic decency had a mouth not becoming of such lineage.

"I said, take your hands off me. I'm not a fucking invalid!"

"I'm so sorry, Madam, I was only meaning to help you to your family," while nodding towards where they all stood (they were still the only ones momentarily left waiting to collect).

"Monty, who the hell have you brought with you? I didn't take part in the World Cup or the Olympics. Why such a reception?"

Once again, all was explained.

Auntie Mildred was not at all happy, but her frustrations soon subsided when Beth had said they had plenty of wine to drink at home and, as soon as she saw Beth's car, she was delighted not to be travelling back amongst the rubbish on Monty's seats.

They made their way home.

"Beth, you drive like a lunatic. Slow down for fuck's sake."

Immediately, Beth obeyed Auntie Mildred's order.

Monty smiled beside his aunt. Beth caught sight of that and stuck out her tongue.

Jordan slept all the way home. The calm before the storm (Storm Mildred).

As they pulled into their driveway, Monty mouthed, "Thank God." He had forgotten just how deep a sleep Auntie Mildred always seemed to fall into. Beth did find herself dying inside. *What the hell makes that kind of noise?* she thought, thankful at the same time that she was married to Jordan and not Auntie Mildred.

Beth was not quite so discreet when she noticed Auntie Mildred had managed to throw her left leg over Monty and now that they had stopped completely, turned to observe the remarkable noise that came from the tiny frame.

Monty was unable to open the door in order to escape because the child safety lock was on and so needed to rely on Beth's assistance, which, much to his annoyance, was taking her far too long. Following her dance across the front of the car, she then proceeded to moonwalk beside the door whilst giving him both middle fingers, which he quickly reciprocated.

"MONTY! They certainly didn't teach you that at Gresham's," bellowed Auntie Mildred, at which point Jordan was instantly brought back to earth from his pleasant land of dreams.

As Beth opened the car door, Monty all but fell out.

"Bitch!"

Beth just laughed and opened the front door.

Auntie Mildred walked straight in leaving Monty and Beth to bring in her luggage, which she didn't want to leave in the car in case the village thieves were lurking.

"It's quite safe here, Auntie Mildred, you're not in Johannesburg now."

"In, please," and she was off to the fridge to find the wine.

Beth had made a steak pie. She couldn't turn her hand to much in the kitchen, unlike Jordan who was a fantastic chef.

Pie, mashed potato and peas – surely that's a hearty meal to come back to (with a glass or two of wine) sitting by the fire. Surely Auntie Mildred would find her happy place and fall back into hopefully a much quieter slumber (for Jordan's sake).

"Let's just eat sitting on the sofa, Monty. Once Auntie Mildred has been to the loo and Jordan's had a shower, we can set off on our adventure. It's half five now and we need to be there for seven. We can walk, it's that close."

As Jordan walked down the stairs, he seemed to remember that he wasn't alone in the house with his wife and retraced his steps to (Beth suspected) put on some underwear beneath his dressing gown.

"Oh, we are eating on the sofa, are we? I suppose it's at least a step up from the floor."

Bloody hell, thought Beth, *you really are Miss Whiplash.*

As they finished eating, the first and only comment about her pie came from Auntie Mildred.

"Steak could have done with another hour. Kept my teeth until I was 88 – doubtful they'll all be there tomorrow."

No, you're not a bitch, you're a– Beth's thoughts were interrupted when Monty coughed without warning and a piece of gristle shot across the floor.

"Time to go." Beth jumped to her feet and went to grab their outdoor ghost hunting clothes.

"Do you have a torch, Beth? And maybe some gloves? I did bring Uncle Joe's Mint Balls for our walk."

"More Like Auntie Mildred's big balls! She most certainly doesn't hold back, does she?"

"The steak *was* a bit tough, Beth. I thought I'd coughed up a lung – pastry was nice though."

"I know, I was rushing though – all I did with the pastry was roll it out. Come on. We'll be late."

As they went into the sitting room to say their goodbyes, Jordan was already asleep on the sofa – thank God he'd put his underpants on.

Auntie Mildred was also asleep – however, she was clinging hold of her wine with a vice-like grip. Monty had tried to remove it from her clutches gently, but she wasn't letting go for anything.

"It is bloody freezing, Beth. Can't we drive?"

"Don't be a dope, Monty. We can climb over the fence and walk through the woods and across the lawn."

"Oh, you rebel! I'm OK with that though. I don't think my right leg is up to a long walk following my experience in the car."

They walked to the fence, Beth began her ascent and within the first two steps, she was thrown back onto the road.

"Oh, crap! It's electrified towards the top. They should have signs saying so."

Monty was sure there would be signs somewhere, but was equally sure that would be an argument she would lose in court.

So, along the very dark, very quiet road, they walked. Once at the gate – which had been opened as they approached – Monty walked (as directed) down the side of the cattle grid. Beth, who had not seen the same sign, balanced her way over the cattle grid until she felt she couldn't make it to the end and crawled across the last 10 or so metal bars.

"How do you get through a day, Beth?" He daren't mention they had passed several signs informing any potential pole vaulters of the high levels of electricity running along the fencing.

Out came the tongue again.

As they walked down the drive, the Hall seemed as far away as it did when they first entered the grounds. The trees lining the driveway seemed quite welcoming with their gently swaying branches, which caused the few remaining leaves to fall to the ground, almost like a carpet welcoming you in.

"Sweet Lord, will we ever get there?" Monty had already had enough.

"We're almost there," which in fact was true. However, Beth did notice the number of cars on the driveway and silently wished they had driven.

Waterdale Hall was huge. Every window was illuminated. *What an electricity bill they must get*, thought Monty, who really only ever put a light on in a room he was in. He was very aware of unnecessary expense and could not understand anyone who was not. Beth was one of the 'was nots'. For her, it wasn't lights – she could have three TVs on at the same time – excusing this because she didn't want to miss anything or risk watching something later only to be told what had happened during one of her multi-Skype chats. She is an 'in the moment' type of girl.

The great doors were open – which led to another set of great doors, which were not.

"Surely you don't have to buzz to get in? That's bonkers when they have invited us." Monty, at this point, was ready to go home.

Beth buzzed in any event.

"I'm sorry, why are you here?" asked the voice on the other side.

"We're here for the ghost hunt," replied Beth, at which point she realised how very Yvette Fielding in *Ghosthunting with...* she sounded.

"How old are we?" asked Monty between retracing of steps. He obviously felt slightly awkward.

"Ghost hunt? Oh, I'm sorry, dear, you need to go to the yard at the back of the house; you're all in the stabling and second cellar area. The main house is hosting a dinner party this evening. For some reason the two events were scheduled on the same evening. Do you know how to find the yard?"

They were directed round the side of the house (which, again, seemed to go on forever – like Diana Dors' legs, according to Beth's mum).

At last, they found the yard. There was a sign written (in Monty's opinion) in a manner not befitting the setting and surroundings:

Ghost Hunt This Way

"OK then." Beth couldn't contain her excitement. "Here we go," she said, switching on her torch and then shining it directly into Monty's face.

"So predictable – turn it off."

Beth just chuckled and told him he needed a filling.

Off they went into the straw-filled room – dark and seemingly very empty.

CHAPTER TWO

"OK, this is weird. Where is everyone?" Beth's excitement seemed to vanish as quickly as it had appeared.

"Some may argue the room is full… of ghosts." Monty was now sure that he had the upper hand. He could see Beth was not best pleased so he took the opportunity to suggest they head back home.

"No way," she said, "there's a second cellar. Let's find it."

Goddam you, Beth! thought Monty.

So, torches on, they looked around the barn finding nothing you wouldn't expect to find in a barn.

"This is absolutely beyond bonkers, Beth, there's nothing here of any interest whatsoever."

"Oh no?" drawled Beth as she opened a door in the far corner of the barn. Her torch revealed some very narrow stone steps.

"This must be the cellar, Monty."

"Beth, I love you. You are my dearest friend, but this is the route to nowhere. Clearly no-one but us is here for this hunt. We don't even have a guide. My guess is they decided to cancel and we just didn't get the e-mail."

Beth wasn't listening. Instead, she was walking with purpose down the steps.

Back at the house, in what should have been the sanctity of his own home, Jordan remembered he was not alone.

Very slowly, he opened one eye and then the other.

Great news! She was still asleep. Not the kind of sleep where you wondered if they had passed away peacefully. A silent sleeper with a little rise and fall. Sadly no, there was zero chance of that.

Where was her volume control?

Twenty-three hours on a flight, the constant droning of the plane engines, which actually provided a degree of solitude – to this.

With the same degree of care he applied to opening his eyes, he gently pulled himself from the sofa to make his way to the fridge where he hoped to find something to drink. Hopefully then, he could drink himself to the same place as Mildred where they could at least compete to piss one another off.

"You can take my glass when you go. I'll go for red this time unless you have another bottle of white, but I couldn't find it earlier…" Auntie Mildred was alive after all.

"Do you want to go to bed, Auntie Mildred?" he asked. In the hope he could create some distance between them, he found himself offering her free lodgings.

"I most certainly do not, young man. I have never been with a man younger than me and I'm not starting at this age." Although, she had to admit, she was flattered and it meant that the hundreds spent on various creams and lotions seemingly were working their magic.

"No, no, I didn't mean with me!" Jordan felt sick even at the thought.

"That's what they *all* say when they're rejected, sweetheart!" Mildred winked at him and took her own glass into the kitchen where she immediately sourced a new bottle of Pinot Noir. The problem with some people is they dither and, at 88, people don't dither.

Not too far away at the Hall, the wine was also flowing. This wine, however, wasn't Berry Bros & Rudd Good Ordinary anything – this was First Growth Bordeaux and anyone who knew anything about wine would certainly know the difference between the two.

The dining hall was awash with land and business owners. Agnes loved to see how the ladies were dressed. She adored beautiful clothes, but on her budget, she wouldn't embarrass herself chasing that particular dream. That said, she had been in town on two separate occasions and paid a visit to the vintage clothes shop where she was sure two of the purchases (the only two she had made) were items once owned by Lady Grey. On that basis alone, how or where could she ever wear them? For now though, she would cast her eyes over future prospects and seemingly she found some satisfaction here.

Lady Grey looked stunning. Tall, slim and toned, she was a truly lovely person. Anyone who worked at the Hall had nothing but respect for her. Her kindness was always evident and she was so humble. No-one ever felt that they worked for her and it was that respect that helped to retain their staff.

Lord Grey, sadly, was not so kind and, my word, didn't you know who you worked for. On many an occasion, the staff wanted to remind him that it was a privilege he married into. This was not his birthright but that of his wife.

He was, in a word, arrogant.

Agnes had been with the family for such a long time that she had almost forgotten how arrogant Lord Grey was, only almost though.

There was one time when she had overheard him telling his wife that they should replace Agnes with a younger, more attractive housekeeper so that when people came to the Hall, they were greeted by an attractive face rather than that of a sad, lonely old woman, who would most likely benefit from a bloody good makeover.

Agnes, although sickened by his cruel words, could hardly offer any argument – she was all of those things, but he missed out that she felt trapped and lonely. She missed her husband following his death, but at least she had Frank and Flora for company and for that she was grateful. Agnes *did* agree with Lord Grey though – she did need some help to transform her appearance.

Lord Grey, as ever, was circulating – usually with the women. The men knew to avoid him. He irritated most of them, but they tolerated him because they respected his wife and, of course, the Greys always provided a 'no expense is spared' party.

Agnes' focus was now upon the two Grey offspring.

Master Felix. It was always with much sadness that Agnes

looked upon this young man.

As a boy, he was sent packing to Gresham's in Norfolk. A great school, but Felix didn't want to go. As a younger boy, he wanted to be with his mother. His father offered him little affection and would, when opportunity knocked, ridicule the huge gap between his front teeth. Several years of train tracks sorted that out and Felix grew into a very handsome young man. Unfortunately though, his social circles were not the kind of people his mother took to.

Felix liked to show off. He would often invite his many friends to the Hall without prior warning. Agnes would be expected to facilitate the extra guests at a moment's notice.

It was from this point that Agnes noticed Felix was beginning to inherit his father's arrogance and other traits that were equally as ugly.

Tonight, however, he seemed relaxed and co-operative in this huge room filled with endless employment opportunities (not that he had ever worked a day in his life).

Then there was Flora. Now, here was a young lady who not only looked serene this evening, but also looked quite unassuming.

Flora shied away from the 'Family Fame'. Having attended Gresham's like her brother, Flora studied like crazy. Knowing that she wanted to work in the medical field but fully aware that she didn't want to be a doctor, she knew she needed to work hard because, academically, she was not as gifted as her brother.

How beautiful she looked. All eyes were upon her – Flora was the pride and joy of her mother's eye. It is true to say that she had no feelings at all for her father. Fully aware of his philandering ways and his sharp tongue, Flora loathed that he was so cruel about so many people who offered nothing but kindness to the family.

Tonight, she behaved just as any other young lady should at a family event, although inside she hated these nights.

Flora spotted Agnes and winked at her. The two of them shared a warm relationship.

Flora would go to the Gate House where Agnes lived and she would tell her all about her day and her work. Agnes had never had children – it was always something both she and her late husband had longed for, but the timing just never seemed right and then it was too late – her husband had died and, at the same time, something inside Agnes died too.

The guests were ordered into the large dining hall. How beautiful it looked. Glasses shining, silverware gleaming. How much hard work that had been. An entire week's work pulling this together and, within no time, it would be over and the next phase of hard work would begin getting the house back in order.

The interesting thing about these types of homes is that they are filled with splendour, glamour and are steeped in history. Just a short distance from all of this, two young people were scratching around in the dust and dirt of the barn. What a contrast this was.

"Monty, you need to see this."

"I don't think I do actually, those steps are stone and steep as hell. Come on, Beth, let's just call it a night and go back for a glass of wine with the others if they are still awake."

"…Beth! BETH!"

Suddenly, Monty, who wasn't that brave, began to feel as though he wasn't alone. When the realisation set in that he was, in fact, on a ghost hunt, he began to believe that he was definitely *not* alone and surprisingly flew down the stairs and proceeded to whack his head on Beth's shoulder, which hurt like a bitch.

"Shit, that hurt!" cried Beth.

"Yes, it bloody did – has anyone ever told you that you have bony shoulders, Beth? I think you pierced my cheekbone."

"I've been using my phone torch to see what's what down here, Monty, and I can see the only way out is through that tunnel in the corner."

"Tunnel? You are joking, obviously. A tunnel is what you drive through to Calais… that's a rabbit hole. Under no circumstances are we crawling through that. It's a complete health and safety risk."

"Monty, please, when do we ever consider health and safety? 'Danger' is our middle name. Besides, this is a proper tunnel, it's all bricked out – I think this is an old escape route – but from where to where – we'll know soon enough."

Monty knew that any defence would be no defence. He was

doomed from this point on; any resistance would be futile.

"Come on, Monty – can't you feel the excitement running through your veins?"

"Well, I can certainly feel something. Not too sure it's excitement though."

Monty laughed. Jokes weren't his forte, but that one really tickled him.

On the face of it, it seemed Beth had either ignored him or hadn't heard him, but the reality was that she was now well and truly into the tunnel. There was a small chintz of light that had caught her attention almost immediately.

Where could that be coming from? This is a tunnel after all – what light could there be along here?

And off she went, gathering pace as she moved on.

Monty, who happened to be sporting a complete bargain (several, actually) from a trendy little Belgravia clothes shop, was not impressed at all.

The bargain trousers in burnt orange, were now absolutely filthy. The knees were almost black.

He recalled collecting the four pairs of trousers and cashmere jumpers feeling completely satisfied that his shrewd negotiation had saved him a fortune.

Bloody Beth and her adventures.

Then, Monty saw the same chintz of light that had caught Beth's eye. He hoped that this meant they would be out of this claustrophobic hellhole within minutes.

"Holy crap! Monty, hurry up – wait till you see this – it's so spooky – I can almost smell danger, can you?"

"That's me, Beth – I'm absolutely shitting myself. I hate confined spaces, I hate the dark, I hate being scared and I hate you. Fucking hell, Beth, what *is* this place? It looks like something a witch would live in."

It actually did. Beth was so excited she could hardly keep it in.

Then, they heard a noise – at first, it sounded like two people having a friendly chat – one of them was laughing, Beth thought.

Monty, who usually didn't pick up on the art of discretion until he'd either been seen or heard, kept surprisingly quiet.

Beth and Monty didn't move; there was no reason initially to feel awkward being there, they had, after all, accepted an invitation to the ghost hunt – the fact that they had mapped out their own route was neither here nor there.

It was something about the tone of the voices that forced them to maintain their silence.

"Why the fuck are you here? Who invited you? You have no right to be here."

"This isn't about having a right, you know why I am here – either you go in there and tell them all about this situation right here or I will."

The voices were quite low, but very clear.

"I will be saying nothing and nor will you."

The second person laughed almost hysterically. The first person remained very quiet.

There was a third person, the only evidence being the number of feet she could see.

Beth moved to look through the crack in the floorboards – she could barely make out the three figures. They were all male and she noticed they were tall, over six feet, although this was a complete guestimate.

Where the people were walking around, the dust that fell from the old wooden flooring fell into her eyes.

Monty, who had anticipated the dusty eye probability, always carried wet wipes and he found himself using the wet wipes to clear his nose. There was no room for a sneeze down here. Certainly not right now. The worst thing that could happen would be for one of them to sneeze – especially when, for some odd reason, they both felt as though they were snooping and ought not be there.

Something made them stay stone-cold still. For Beth, she wanted to know what was going to happen next. For Monty, he just couldn't see the way out – where was the exit sign? He was looking around for the green and white exit light you see at the cinema. Why? This was hardly Cineworld, although he did feel like he was in a film.

"Listen, you have one option here, you go upstairs and you tell them or I promise you I will. I haven't travelled all this way to go back, not having carried out what I intended to do."

"You have no idea how bad your situation is. You have no idea the trouble you are in because the people you have upset know people and they are not people you need to be on the wrong side of."

"Fuck off!" The tone of the older person was pretty final and the younger man didn't appear to be that old from what Beth could see. In truth though, she was struggling to see anything conclusive. The third person spoke now.

"You really are going to cause a huge problem for yourself if you don't leave right now, I can promise you that."

Beth touched Monty's arm – it was all he could do not to scream. She knew he had a nervous disposition.

"Is that a knife? Why do you have a knife? This house is filled with so many people – how do you think you are going to explain this to everyone?"

"I'm going to say this one last time; go home, forget you came here and stay out of this."

"That is not something I can do. That is not something I *will* be doing."

"Then you leave me with no choice…"

The talking stopped and, other than the few steps towards the second person, the only sound was a stifled whimper and a thud.

The man's body fell to the floor and did not move. The knife (Beth presumed he had used the knife) was clearly inserted in a spot that the user knew would be fatal.

Monty, who knew to keep his hands over his mouth, looked up to see what Beth was seeing, at which point, the blood ran freely through another crack in the wood and down Monty's face and neck.

Uncomfortable even at the sight of blood, his unimaginable urge to cry out, vomit, anything actually, to express his horror of what was happening right now, was overshadowed by the consequence of any of these reactions if they were to be heard.

They heard footsteps and knew that they had a very short amount of time to get out of the room they were in before they were either discovered or trapped. Neither of them wanted to be in the room when the next series of events upstairs took place.

No words were needed. Beth quickly shone her phone torch around the room. Thankfully, she spotted in the far corner a small door, the handle looked almost non-existent, but this was her preferred choice of escape rather than to backtrack – who knew about this place? A great place to store a body until you could think of an alternative resting place.

What just happened would change everything. Who was the person who was killed and who was the killer?

Already, Beth was in sleuth mode; this time though, it wasn't a story she had invented in her head, this was real. Someone actually died. Spending years putting herself in this very situation, the drama, the excitement almost – this was not how she had imagined it to be. This is real and it is happening. She had to think and remain calm. How could she possibly tell Monty that she, too, wanted to be sick? She was scared to death.

Beth was responsible for putting her friend in this situation. He had never had the dreams she had. Knowing she had to get them both out of there, she put all her feelings aside and scoured the room for a safe escape route.

Slowly, she and Monty (who was clinging on to Beth as a child would cling to its mother) moved over to the corner where the door was. Beth felt that she needed to say something to Monty – reassurance, comfort or both. Fully aware that she was the stronger of the two mentally, she needed to take charge of this situation and think only of getting them out safely and as quickly as possible.

The door, although falling to bits, opened relatively easily. It led to another tunnel, but a slightly higher one than the last.

Both walking slightly bent over given the head room, in silence, they made their way down the second tunnel. They had obviously no idea where they were going, but the fact they were heading away from the crime they had witnessed, Beth felt was the safest option.

They walked for about half a mile stopping only to lie down

and stretch themselves out, but neither of them said a single word. Beth could hear her heart beating, Monty could feel his beating in his ears, his chest and his throat, but even he had to admit, they needed to get the hell out of there and quickly. The maze they were following seemed endless and they found themselves going from standing, to crouching and then crawling.

Neither of them could imagine the thought processes of the people who had made these tunnels – couldn't they all be the same height? This had to be a problem for anyone, even hundreds of years ago, surely.

Finally, they saw a set of metal ladders up against the wall at the end of the tunnel. Beth's only worry now was where they would lead.

In the hope that they wouldn't open up in the house given the distance they'd walked, she told Monty to stay where he was as she climbed up almost 30 steps to the top of the ladder.

Not known for her physical strength, Beth couldn't seem to push her way out. In truth, there was no way of knowing if there was a bolt on the other side.

Realising the enormity of the situation growing each minute and the knowledge that Monty had even less chance of blasting their way out, this was on her.

With one last effort, she pushed, thinking as she did so, of her beloved Jordan. The thought of being found on the wrong side of this door left Beth under no illusion that they would be in grave trouble.

It was with a creak and some very slow progress that the door began to open. Beth could feel the air on her face, so she knew that they were somewhere outside – where exactly that was, she had no clue.

From nowhere, and with very little room, Monty was beside her, pushing with everything that made him.

The lid became as wide as it needed to be to allow them to crawl out.

They found themselves in the middle of some trees.

Beth was shaking. She began to cry. Monty closed the lid again

– noticing it seemed to close much easier than it had opened.

"Shit, bloody shit!" Beth groaned. "My phone – where's my phone?"

No time to think about that. They heard voices.

Monty, who for the first time that day, took charge, forced both himself and Beth face down on the ground.

The voices, thankfully, were quite cheery and spoke of the enormity of the clearing up process following the party. One of the girls said she loved clearing up after a large party because she took home some of the unopened bottles of wine. Others agreed and they continued to walk right past the two of them on the ground within the coverage of the trees.

"The party can't be over yet, Monty – it's only half nine. Where could they have been going?"

"Who cares, Beth?" Monty stood up and took stock of his surroundings – even though he had no clue where he was.

Beth, however, *did* know where they were. The house was almost 400 metres away; they appeared to be on the other side of the house from the road. She concluded (just to satisfy her own curiosity) that the group of young people had been part of the first shift.

"I think we need to walk towards the house, but along the treeline so that we don't veer off and end up near the house. If we keep walking through the trees, we should end up beside the road."

They walked, Beth thinking about her phone. What if it was found and identified as belonging to her? At some point, she knew she would have to go back down there and find it.

In the meantime, they walked in the pitch dark and in complete silence. It was odd that neither of them spoke about what they had just witnessed. It was almost as though the very mention of it would make it real and, until they returned to Beth's house that was the last thing either of them wanted it to be.

CHAPTER THREE

SAFELY HOME

They found the road and, rather than try to scale what stood between them and the main road for fear of electrocution, they walked towards the gate.

"Beth, we can't walk through the gate, the cameras will pick us up."

"There is no other way, Monty, we just have to be bold and walk out as we walked in. Oh, bloody hell, Monty – look at you!"

Now that it was lighter, both from the moon and the lighting around the perimeter of the house and Gate House, Beth could see for the first time that Monty was covered in blood. His face, neck and, in fact, his upper body were splattered.

Monty now realised that the dried, crusty feeling to his face and the crispness of his hair was the dried blood. Not being able to see for himself, but imagining how this looked, he took to his knees. He thought he was going to pass out.

"I need a minute, Beth. Please give me that. I actually feel so sick and I don't think I can stand up just yet."

"You can't walk out like that, Monty. No way, there's no chance you'll be able to talk your way out of that. Wait, I *do* know there's a small gap in the wall where they used to have a little gate. I think the previous owner had a secret little love gate put in. When it was re-fenced, I think that little gap was missed – I've seen it when I've been walking."

About-turn and off they went in search for the little gap.

And there it was – and it was indeed a little gap. Beth pushed herself through, thankful that she was not gifted with large breasts. Monty, meanwhile, whilst of slight build, caught his bargain cashmere jumper on a thorn and instantly created a hole.

"Piss and piss. Look at this hole, Beth."

Unimaginably, Beth laughed.

"Monty, you are covered in the blood of a dead man. A dead man who was murdered right above us. Please don't worry about a fucking hole. Seriously – get a grip! Do you actually know you are covered in blood?"

Monty threw up.

They could see Beth's house now. It was about a half-mile up the road. This would be half a mile that would take forever to cover.

The door opened – Jordan hadn't locked it. Perhaps he was still up. If he was, Beth decided that she would need to go back to find her phone.

They would need to stay calm right now. How could they avoid Auntie Mildred overhearing any of this? She seemed to Beth to be someone who could not keep anything to herself other than her money (according to Monty).

Above all else, Monty had to get into the shower and get himself into some clean clothes.

He needed little persuasion to do this.

When he came downstairs, Beth was sitting drinking wine at the kitchen table. Having established nothing would wake up her exhausted husband, she had decided to leave him to sleep and, thankfully, Auntie Mildred wasn't waking up any time soon – exhaustion and around two bottles of wine (and that was just since she'd got here) put paid to consciousness.

Monty didn't speak to Beth, instead, he got himself a glass and, rather than share Beth's bottle, he got one of his own.

They sat at either end of the table looking at each other.

"I mean, I was happy doing my own thing in London. Yes, Auntie was an inconvenience, but no-one would have fucking died right above my head! Do you know, I have never sworn so much in my life. A bloody ghost hunt, you said! What happens now, Beth? What do we do? We have to report this to the police, you know that, right?"

"I have to get my phone first, Monty. I know that us being there was completely innocent, but we have no idea what they were arguing about; we don't know who the two of them were. We only know there was a knife and a death. How do we know that he's even dead? If we go to the police now, what if they go there and there's been a major clean-up? No-one is missing and we live here, right across the road; how do we deal with that?"

"Beth, no-one bleeds like that and lives. What did you do with my clothes? They will want those, they are evidence."

"Monty, I want to get my phone. I *need* it. It's just all my photos are on there, people I've loved and lost. I can't not have it."

"Look, I get it, Beth, but I can't go back with you. Honestly, I just can't do it. Wait until tomorrow and Jordan can go with you."

"Absolutely not. It needs to be in the dark and now I know how to get in, I can be in and out quite easily. It can only be at the bottom of the steps or very close to them. The only problem I will have is pulling the lid open to get in. What if we wait a couple of hours and go with enough time while it's still dark?"

"WE? Oh no, no, no, no, no! Hopefully, you get that Beth. I don't think either of us really understands or appreciates what we have seen tonight. I have to say, even by your Nancy Drew standards, this was not what I had thought tonight would be. I thought I'd be carting madam off to her pad right now and look where we are."

"How do we keep this from her, Monty? She cannot know. You know she'll be talking to the press and everyone who'll listen to her."

"Look, you leave her to me and you sort out your phone. I'll get her home and then come back – I'll need to be here when the police come round. You know they'll ask you why you left it so long to call them."

"I know – one of the reasons I want to go back is to see if there's anything I can fathom out about what happened – see if things have been moved. See if the body is still there."

None of this made sense. None of this seemed real. How does anyone behave rationally when they've been through something like this?

"OK, Monty, I'll wait for Jordan. Let's get some sleep." Neither did, they sat and drank another bottle and talked for an hour or so until they heard someone coming downstairs.

Both Beth and Monty hoped they were Jordan's footsteps, which thankfully, they were.

"OK, guys, two questions – where the hell have you been? Why didn't you come to bed, Beth? And actually, one more question, who the bloody hell thought it was a good idea for me to babysit that bossy old cow?" Jordan was mad.

"We came home and you hadn't locked the door."

"No? That, my love, was more wishful thinking than absent-mindedness. I was wishing that someone would come in and take her away. She snores like an animal I don't believe has walked the earth for millions of years, but yet, grab yourself a drink and miss her out, she just knows. Wait a minute; what's the deal here? Neither of you has been to bed, you were still out at one am because I came downstairs to check. I called you, Beth, but you didn't pick up."

"Fucking hell, tell me you didn't!" Beth said, realising how this could be so problematic for her.

"Of course I did, that's what people do when they are worried about their loved ones – are you going to tell me what's happened? Why is me calling you a problem?"

"Jordan, it's just after five and I need you to come with me. I don't have time to tell you right now what's happened, I'll do that when we leave the house. Monty, you know what you need to do. I'll see you as soon as you get back. Go and wake up the kraken. Tell her what you need to and just get back here."

"Beth, where are we going out now? What's happened?"

"Seriously, Jordan, let's do this when we're walking."

"Beth, where did you put my clothes? We will need them."

"Leave them with me, Monty. Just get rid of her."

Monty said nothing more. Beth looked at Jordan while she was pulling on her short boots. Jordan also said nothing else but, inside, he had the feeling that whatever he was about to hear was not going to be good. He knew his wife.

Nothing, however, could have prepared him for what he was about to hear.

CHAPTER FOUR

WHAT JUST HAPPENED

As they walked, Beth surprised herself with her control. She has always been credited for her ability to remain calm when those around her were not. Literally, from the time she and Monty left the house until they got back home, Jordan heard every detail.

He too remained very calm. It was most likely disbelief that helped him right now. He was used to his wife and her Miss Marple antics – ghosts, ghouls and the like. Beth was an old- fashioned head in a young body. He had always loved that about her, but now, right in this moment, she was anything but herself. Jordan knew that this was as serious as she was saying it was.

"We need to go back down there, Jordan. I need to find my phone. You see why I freaked out when you said you'd called me?" Which of course he did.

"Why not just call the police, Beth? Why go back to who knows what we are going to find or, most worryingly, who we will find down there?"

"To be honest, Jordan, I'm hoping that he isn't dead. I'm hoping that he was badly injured, but is alive and that the family are sorting out this whole matter. That way, we need not mention we were even there."

"Do you even know where this lid is, Beth? It sounds like a pretty small target area in a large space."

"I have a good idea but, no, I don't know exactly where it is."

They walked around for about half an hour once they had managed to get Jordan through the gap in the fencing. Daylight wasn't too far away, but Beth did also make out a rather large cow not too far away. She'd forgotten about them.

It was actually Jordan who found the lid. It was a complete fluke that he did, but all things considered, this wasn't about point-scoring, although Beth did high five him without thinking.

The lid was not an easy challenge. It was definitely harder to lift than it had been to push – maybe their strength came from fear, but either way, both Beth and Jordan were pulling hard when finally they felt it give in to them. She seemed to remember Monty felt that it closed easier – she decided that was the strength in fear.

Jordan looked at Beth. Without saying a word, Beth knew he was thinking, *OK, what now?*

"Have you brought *your* phone, Jordan?"

"No, did I need it?"

"Only for the torch."

Jordan pulled out his little tool thing that he took everywhere – within the mechanics of this small device, he switched on the torch, which was pointing down the hole.

"Miners always carry a torch. That is quite some way down there, Beth. Are you sure about this?"

"No," came the reply, "but I have no choice and, besides, I want to make sure that this isn't real and what we thought we saw was just something that wasn't quite as bad as it had looked."

Down they climbed. Beth went first, Jordan maintaining his duty as torch bearer. He was in awe of his wife's bravery, but at the same time, he didn't really comprehend what had gone on. How could he? All of this going on while he entertained the fire-breathing dragon.

They walked along the passage, which seemed to take much longer than it had earlier.

Jordan did correct Beth in so much as you couldn't count this as a walk. For him, it was definitely more of a crawl. The silence was deafening – people say that and you think that's just rubbish, but the silence was so loud it was freaking him out. Beth, however, carried on and so must he.

Finally, they reached the opening. The oddest thing was that from the moment they had gotten into the tunnel, she had forgotten to look for her phone. She was more intent on seeing the room again. Beth did question whether this was the real reason she wanted to come back.

"Jordan, shine the torch around the room."

Nothing, absolutely nothing in that room suggested they had been there. There was no blood, the floorboard was completely clean – certainly from underneath. The body – or the person whom she had thought was dead – was no longer there.

They looked at each other. Beth felt relief like she had never known. Wait until she told Monty. Then, with a bit of stitching and a good old handwash, his jumper would be back in service. Everything would be back in place.

Shouldn't she even question what had happened with the people who owned the Hall? No, she decided. She would wait to see if there were any local whispers. Jordan, however, felt differently, but of course, he hadn't seen the before, only the after and he knew how sometimes his wife's imagination worked overtime.

"OK, let's get out of here and one things for sure, your phone isn't here in this room – I've scoured it. Did you have it in here?"

"Yes, for sure."

"Well, it must be in the tunnel – we'll have to have a good look on the way back."

They looked the entire way out of the tunnel. No phone. Jordan suggested it was probably on the grass outside. Beth agreed that that was the most likely place it could be.

Once back in the fresh air, morning almost upon them, they looked everywhere around the lid area. Again, nothing!

As odd as it was that they couldn't find the phone, such was Beth's relief that they didn't need to deal with the other matter, The Murder, she decided that she would report the phone as lost, close everything down and get herself another phone.

She was due one after all.

Back at the house, Monty and Auntie Mildred had left, only just, was Beth's guess since the kettle was still quite warm and the toaster had a slice of toast in it, which was still warm-ish.

They had obviously left in haste – that would have been Monty's choice, so there would be absolutely no way his aunt would be around for any chatting and possible intrusion.

"OK," said Jordan, "please can we sit down and discuss this without any fear of being interrupted, so that I am able to understand what actually went on last night. With or without a body, Beth, you did witness something quite appalling and you do not know for sure that this person survived what you had witnessed."

Beth could feel the relief she had felt earlier fall away. Jordan was absolutely right. Something terrible *did* happen and it was her wishful thinking that everything was OK and that perhaps the man got up and shook hands with his attacker.

This was unusual for Beth; she had spent her life dramatizing events, turning them into potential 'sightings' or ghoulish mysteries that she could solve with her trusty pal, Monty.

Deep down, she knew that, finally, all the years of hoping for something to happen, for her to be in the wrong place at the wrong time, happened last night and now, rather than getting her notepad out, she was keen to sweep it aside and pretend nothing had happened. An eventless evening. A ghost hunt without the ghost.

Beth and Jordan both sat nursing their cups of tea. No-one said a word. This was mostly because neither one knew what to say.

All of a sudden, and without any warning at all, Monty walked through the kitchen door. He looked like death. In truth, this analogy was truer than any other – Beth should know what death looked like – shouldn't she?

Monty really didn't look good.

"Fucking hell!"

He walked to the fridge and pulled out a bottle of white wine, surprisingly still half full despite Auntie Mildred having stayed overnight.

He too sat down, exclaiming nothing more than that.

It was Jordan who spoke next.

"OK, guys, break this right down for me, please, from the time you left the house until you walked back through that door right there."

It had been Monty who took the reins. He was more detailed than Beth had ever known him to be – right until the point of the attack, then he stopped in his tracks.

"He dropped to the floor, Jordan, like a lead weight, and all I could see was his eye staring at me and the blood seeped through the wooden floor."

The whole dynamic had changed in 24 hours.

Jokes, laughter and lighthearted banter. It had all gone.

The actions of someone else had affected their lives.

"Did you find your phone?" Monty wasn't even looking at her. He was pouring himself another glass of wine.

"No."

"Holy crap – supposing they find it down there?" Still pouring.

"If it *was* there, they found it already. We looked everywhere. Nothing."

"Have you given any thought to what happens if that's the case?"

"No, Monty, I haven't. I'm so tired. I need to sleep."

"I think we *all* need sleep. Monty, are *you* tired?"

"I'm completely fucked, Jordan. Auntie didn't stop bloody talking all the way to drop-off. I couldn't even engage with her. Drop-off – drive back. Let's all have a sleep and hopefully we can at least think clearly afterwards."

They managed to take themselves upstairs to bed. Monty carried his half bottle of wine with him. Everyone needed some company and this was to be his right now.

Beth and Jordan, who are typically very tactile, just went to bed – neither of them getting changed. Jordan had at least slept last night, but the strain of what he had been through these past few hours, plus the jetlag that he hadn't slept off completely, was beginning to take its toll.

Beth was already asleep. Jordan was grateful that she had managed to drop off – it's never easy when you have such enormity weighing heavy on your shoulders.

Monty, bless him, was most probably the first to find sleep. He wasn't used to this type of day-to-day living (excluding the whatever it was that had happened). The most he had to deal with was usually the homeless lady whom he had grown quite fond of, close to Waitrose. He would buy her food on a more than he liked regular basis, but he found her challenging. He did see the funny side, though – that this homeless old lady whom he'd been feeding chocolate to could justify criticising his lifestyle. What a life coach! He could hardly go anywhere else to shop; he had a loyalty card, so it made sense. Surely she could find another doorway. He composed himself and remembered that she probably looked forward to seeing him. Right now, he would love for her to be his one and only thought as he fell asleep. He needn't have worried, sleep found him pretty quickly.

It was almost dark when they eventually surfaced. Beth had decided they would eat and talk things through, as they did.

Jordan was the first in the kitchen, followed by Monty (with an empty bottle) – even he couldn't work out how that had happened.

Beth made up the rear. As she reached the bottom of the stairs, she felt herself tense and a wave of anxiety wafted over her. What the hell had they got themselves into?

Certain of at least one thing, she would buy her new phone. Terminate the old number and everything with it. Hopefully terminating every memory of last night. Not too sure how quickly she would be able to lock out anyone who discovered it, she could only hope that it would be a swift process; however, this couldn't be her focus right now.

The doorbell rang.

"I'll get it," Beth managing to voice at least that much.

Opening the door, she didn't know whom she expected to see. There was no-one there. Walking down the three steps from the front door, no-one was walking or driving in either direction.

As she turned to go back into the house, she saw a small, brown box.

Taking it inside, certain that it was a delivery for Jordan, she walked into the kitchen.

Putting the box onto the table, she saw, for the first time, her name written on the top.

Looking from Jordan to Monty, then back at the box, she

flipped the lid open.

A card, very expensive but completely blank, lay on top of whatever lay beneath.

As she lifted the card from the box, she immediately saw her phone.

Written on the reverse of the card, in the same pen as her name had been written…

'I believe this belongs to you. How careless.'

They all looked at one another.

Now their conversation would take a completely different turn.

CHAPTER FIVE

"Who's that?" Beth was disturbed by the sound of a motorbike.

"Oh no," said Monty so quietly it was almost a whisper.

"What?" said Jordan.

"I may be wrong, I hope I am; however, that sounds very much like Auntie Mildred's motorcycle."

Jordan laughed, almost dismissing what he had heard.

"Beth!"

Yes, it was indeed Auntie Mildred. Why was she shouting for Beth?

Instinctively, Beth ran outside to find this dear old lady clambering off her motorcycle (Betsy).

"Hi Auntie Mildred, can't you stay away?"

"Grab that bag, it's too heavy for me."

There are two men inside, thought Beth, as she attempted to pick up the bag, which, as per the description, was so heavy.

"What the hell do you have in here, Auntie Mildred?"

"Wine – I can't drink that rubbish in your fridge again."

"Quite possibly because you've guzzled all bar one bottle – Monty's had the last bottle so it would either be red or coffee."

"Oh, hello Jordan, there's supplies in there, Beth. There are a couple of things I picked up on my last trip, I think they'll look lovely on you. I thought we could go out for dinner. I stopped by the pub, lovely little place; I managed to get us a table. Half an hour, guys, so chop-chop!"

"Monty, darling, surprise!"

"Two things, Auntie Mildred: how did you know I'd be here? And what are you doing here so soon?"

"Well, I have something to tell you and I didn't want to do it on the phone."

So, they were going to The Inglenook.

Three of the four were surprised for a whole host of reasons.

What is she doing back so soon? It is remarkably out of character for her, thought Monty.

What the hell did she have to tell them that they needed a face to face meeting?

And finally, how the hell has she manage to get a table at no notice, in a pub that is really fab and tables are typically in short supply?

In some kind of robotic fashion, they all changed (Beth even wore one of the tops Auntie Mildred had bought for her). It was lovely and Beth, despite everything that had happened during the past 24 hours, walked out of the house feeling pretty good about her appearance.

Nothing seemed real.

As they walked into the pub, Burt (the landlord) made a beeline for them. Clearly Auntie Mildred had done a number on him – he was an unfortunate-looking chap – very red faced, which everyone believed to be the levels of alcohol that ran through his veins. His ill-fitting clothes did not flatter him from any angle. From the front, his hairy belly hung beneath his shirt that really battled to contain his full stomach. From the back and, at first glimpse, he looked quite well covered, that was until he bent over, at which point the crack of his bottom made an appearance. Once, a child dropped garden peas down there. Everyone in the pub laughed so loud. That was until Burt retrieved the peas and ate them.

All of that said, the food here was delightful and the pub itself was outstanding. The staff were all lovely and Burt, on a good day, was a very good host.

"Mildred, you came. Come to the bar; let's have drinks before you eat."

Burt often invited himself into the conversations of others.

"No thanks, Burt, I need to speak with these lovely people around a table. Could you ask someone to bring the drinks over, please? That shirt doesn't fit you, Burt. Either buy a bigger one or lose some weight."

"More of me to love, Mildred," as he winked at her.

Walking over to the bar, Mildred pretended to vomit, which was quite funny and they all laughed as discreetly as they could.

They sat down and the drinks came.

"OK, you three, I want to know what's going on?" she said, with her voice rising at the end.

Suddenly, everything came flooding back.

"What do you mean, Auntie?" asked Monty in an almost childlike voice.

"Monty, I am old, not stupid. I saw something last night that has troubled me, but not as much as the journey home this morning. Prisoners have been escorted out of jail with more consideration than you gave to me. You didn't talk any of the way home and you literally shoved me out of the car. You didn't ask if I had any spare wine so I knew you were not staying at home. I guessed what I saw last night might have something to do with you coming back here. So, my young friends, am I right?"

"Well, Auntie Mildred, that depends on what you think you saw."

"No, Jordan, I don't *think* I saw anything, I know I saw *some*thing."

The four of them sat and looked at one another in absolute silence. Who would be the first to speak?

"Bloody hell, Auntie Mildred, I think something really bad happened last night, but I can't be sure, Monty can't be sure and poor old Jordan was dragged into something he still has no idea about."

"Someone died, didn't they." This wasn't a question, it was a statement.

"That, we do not know. Quite possibly yes, but we have no evidence of this."

"Well, I do," said Auntie Mildred matter-of-factly, in a very calm and quiet voice.

"Talk me through what happened from the minute you left,

right up until now."

It was predictably Beth who relayed the entire sequence of events.

"But how can you know anything, Auntie Mildred, when you were in bed all night?"

"Not quite all night. I got up at some ridiculous hour. I could hear you talking in the kitchen. I didn't disturb you – I went to the car to get my pills, but it was locked. As I turned around to go in, I could hear voices across the road in the trees. I couldn't make out what was being said, but I did walk over there and could just about make out two figures. They said they would need to come back to deal with it in the morning, that they needed to deal with the room first."

"I had no idea what was going on, but since I couldn't see a thing and had no way of illuminating anything, I decided I'd go back at first light."

"So, I didn't bother to get dressed, I sat and waited for dawn to break. As I walked out of the house, I saw the two of you walking into the trees so I knew something had to have happened. I walked over to the edge of the wall and through the trees I could see someone lying on the ground. They didn't look well at all."

Auntie Mildred, in her usual manner, beckoned a waitress. Given her education and supposed finishing school etiquette, Beth did wonder at what point in her life she laid that particular chapter in her life to rest. Mildred was, without doubt, the rudest person Beth had ever met. That said, she was also one of the most interesting. Observing her as she found herself doing quite often in her company, she decided most of her characteristics were completely put on.

Beneath that exterior layer of frost and then ice lay a warm, elderly lady who probably longed for a simple life and, Beth suspected, someone to share it with (as long as he didn't mind being ordered around for the rest of his life).

"How can I help you, Madam?" This waitress was clearly new to the job – even though Beth and Jordan were new to the area, Beth could tell she was very young and was probably about to encounter the worst customer ever.

"Well, young lady, working in a pub offering food, your offer of assistance would be twofold; we either need food or drink and since we have neither, take your pick."

They were all wrong!

And back came the reply, "Madam, you are quite right, our services do extend to both food and drink; you finished your drinks two minutes ago. I know that because I cleared your glasses away. For one, you drink far too quickly, and for two, I asked you if you were dining with us and if I should get you some menus. You told me to wait until you had finished speaking – which I did. Now, Madam, same again for drinks? And here are the menus."

Auntie Mildred said only, "Yes, same again; I'll have–"

"Don't worry, I know what you had. Give me a minute."

"Well, you're a sharp cookie, aren't you?" Auntie Mildred then shocked the entire table and the young waitress by winking at her and then smiling.

Silently, the other three decided that was how to speak with Auntie Mildred moving forward. Monty, however, knew that he could never be so brave.

"Let's order food."

They ordered, drank and ate.

Auntie Mildred was convinced they had buried a body within the trees. Jordan, still in complete shock by this whole episode, said that if they had, they need only find the earth that was freshly dug up.

So, a plan was decided upon.

That night, Auntie Mildred would stand at the same point by the wall and Monty and Jordan would go to look in the trees.

Beth, it was decided (and this was much against her will) would be the look out – Monty was far too likely to continue drinking and fall asleep, potentially exposing their entire evening's work.

As they got up to leave, Burt ambled by and asked Auntie Mildred if she would care to join him for another drink once they had closed for the evening.

"I'll pass, thanks, Burt," and off she walked.

Burt, still reeling from the obvious rejection, pulled up his trousers (which immediately sank back below his belly folds), smoothed his few remaining hairs across his head and moved on to another table.

Outside, it was a beautiful evening. The air had thinned and, once more, their thoughts were drawn to the 'body' and what had happened to it.

They walked back home in absolute silence. The darkness seemed complete. Where was the moon? In fact, this was good. Camouflaged by the blackness had to be perfect for what they had planned.

It would be equally beneficial to anyone listening in on their conversation, so their silence was universally accepted right now.

Approaching the house, which Beth loved above anything other than her husband, Monty thought he could see something move by the garage door. Initially, he brushed it off until he saw it again; this time, Beth saw it too.

They stopped. Thankfully, they hadn't stepped onto the gravel, so they were unnoticed.

The figures didn't come back into any kind of view. A couple of minutes went by and Monty walked to the gates, crunching as he went.

Nothing more was seen or heard of the mystery mover.

In the house, they sat round a table and discussed times, clothing, tools and access where Beth would be, to make sure they were not to be seen.

The wine was flowing (much to Beth's disgust). As night watchman, she had to remain focused.

One am came around very quickly. Monty, Jordan and Beth stood in the kitchen dressed in dark jeans, dark shoes and equally dark coats.

Auntie Mildred walked in to the kitchen and, before any of them could stop to think about the seriousness of the situation, they all laughed out loud.

Auntie Mildred stood in black leggings, gloves, short boots and a black jumper. Nothing too funny about that until you saw her head, or rather you didn't see her head for it was covered completely by a black balaclava. Not one that any of them had seen before – it covered her entire face, even her eyes.

"Fucking hell, Auntie Mildred," cried Monty, "you look like a ninja warrior!"

Beneath whatever material she was wearing came a whimper of a chuckle.

"Do you know," she began, "I bought this 15 years ago in Cape Town when I was going to a fancy dress. I never found it, but when I went home earlier, I picked up my old bag that could cope with the jogging of the motorbike and there it was. I am meant to wear this tonight."

"What the hell is that in your hand?" asked Jordan.

What looked like a pair of ladies' tights seemed to be wrapped around her hand, but the end of whatever it was she was holding seemed to be heavy looking.

"Well, I saw this in a film; it's a cosh. If someone startles me, they'll get it."

Again, Jordan's head was spinning. How much had happened since his arrival from Oz. The flight had been filled with all sorts of nice thoughts about what they were going to do to their new home. Who could have thought up any of this?

Beth took her position sitting on the church bench. This sat beneath the oak tree, but she could see and hear from most directions without being seen herself. She had decided to wrap a scarf around her face; if nothing else, she was supporting the Auntie Mildred look.

Auntie Mildred found the stick she had put in the wall to make sure she had the right position while Monty and Jordan crawled through the gap in the hedge – which was obviously a different gap since neither remembered the boulder sticking up that seemed to fight with Monty's jumper beneath his coat. Jordan was through, but he could hear Monty cursing as quietly as he could, but even so, it was obvious he was wrestling with something that had ruined his 100% cashmere sweater – still, he had this one in most colours, but thankfully tonight his orange version stayed indoors.

Jordan used his special torch given to him by one of the miners – it focused just on the area you pointed at rather than illuminating a huge area.

They combed the area – guided by a whispering Auntie Mildred.

They found nothing.

"This is exactly where I stood and that's exactly where they were. Look right by the trees. I read that people use those areas because animals, often foxes, dig around them, so the newly dug out area doesn't look particularly suspicious."

Again, they looked.

Nothing.

Suddenly, Beth was aware of something very close to her. She was lying along the entire bench. It was obvious to her that she was completely hidden. Beth was thankful for the scarf, which she felt suppressed her noisy breathing that was becoming increasingly more irregular.

There were two people. She could just about make out two figures, but neither spoke.

One pointed, but Beth couldn't make out at what.

They moved along.

How could she alert Mildred who was clearly in their path?

All of a sudden, Beth heard two noises. The first was Auntie Mildred who cried out in pain.

The second was (she thought) a man's cries.

Light footsteps ran past her. There were definitely two people.

No-one said anything, but they all made their way back to the house.

It was clear Auntie Mildred had been hurt but, again, no-one said anything. All of them wanted to get back into the safety of their home.

CHAPTER SIX

Neither Jordan nor Monty had seen a thing. They had both been crouching down looking for clues so they were behind the wall.

They had, however, heard movement from the other side of the wall and both cries. Clearly only one of them was Auntie Mildred. They ran back to the hole in the hedge – this time Monty navigated his way through and over the boulder.

As soon as they were on the road, they assumed both Auntie Mildred and Beth had gone into the house.

In the kitchen, they found Beth bathing Auntie Mildred's head, which was covered in blood.

"I'm calling the police," said Monty.

"No, you are not," said Auntie Mildred. Her voice was very firm. "This evening's events have changed things. I need to think."

Beth was already thinking.

Something happened only a short time ago, but so much had happened since, it seemed like an eternity had passed by.

What the hell *did* happen in that room? Logic suggested that the man she saw had been killed.

Auntie Mildred definitely saw something that was connected to what had gone on.

Now this.

Were they being watched? How could anyone know what they had planned for that night?

Wait a minute – the phone.

It had been returned as a warning.

"Auntie Mildred," Beth said in an equally stern tone, "I'm driving you to the hospital. Put on some normal clothes; I'll do the same and, boys, when we get back, we sleep. Then, we work out what the bloody hell to do next."

Beth and Auntie Mildred drove to the hospital.

Auntie Mildred wouldn't shut up. Beth put this down to adrenaline. Beth didn't speak, for there was no need as Auntie Mildred didn't pause for breath and Beth had nothing to say. She was lost in her own thoughts.

At the hospital, Beth said her aunt had walked into the garage door that was left open, in the dark.

They were told to take a seat and wait until they were called.

Both had one thing only on their mind – if Auntie Mildred was in here with her injury, surely the person she whacked would be in here too.

Other than two drunks and one chap who had been involved in a minor road accident, that was it.

"Mildred Broadbent?" a voice called out.

"Broadbent? Who's that?" asked Auntie Mildred.

"I don't know your surname, sorry – Broadbent was my great-aunt's surname."

When she was asked to give her address, Beth had given hers and had to make up Auntie Mildred's surname.

"Well, there's been a lot going on in your neck of the woods tonight. You're the second one we've had in from your village."

So, the person who was hit *had* been in.

The nurse interrupted their thoughts.

"Hi, what have you been up to? Oh, we are neighbours. Wow, I never see anyone from the village. I'm Flora."

Before Auntie Mildred could say a word, Beth stepped in. "She's only just moved in. Where do you live?"

"I live in Waterdale Hall. I'd like to move more into the town but haven't managed to take the plunge just yet. So, you walked into a garage door? Bit late to be doing that, isn't it?"

"Oh, she did it a few hours ago. I'm staying with her, so she waited until I got back in. I thought I could clean it up and she'd be OK, but it's too deep."

"Did you say Waterdale Hall?" asked Auntie Mildred. "The big house."

"Yes, that's right. My parents own it. It's been in the family for ever, pretty much."

"I expect you had some wild adventures as a child, didn't you? Do you have many brothers and sisters?"

Auntie Mildred's fishing, thought Beth.

Auntie Mildred had one eye open and the other closed and swollen. She looked very fragile like this.

Beth found herself to be quite protective of her right now.

"Auntie Mildred, please let the nurse do what she needs to do so that we can get you home. You haven't slept at all tonight."

Flora, Beth decided, was quite lovely. She had a lovely way about her and demonstrated a kindness, which Beth found endearing. The last nurse she had had dealings with was her dentist's nurse and Beth sensed she could kill you with one stare. Beth didn't like her one bit and so this was yet another advantage of moving house – a new dentist.

She must remember to book herself and Jordan in.

"All done, Mildred. You must remember not to drive for a week, I'd say. I've got some strong painkillers for you because this will hurt like hell tomorrow. Beth, is that your niece's name?" she asked as she smiled at Beth. "Here's my number, I'm literally across the road. If you need me, give me a call. I tend to live with our housekeeper in the Gate House, so it's no trouble to come over to you."

"Oh, that's really kind of you, Flora. I'll stay on for a couple of weeks to make sure she's OK."

Beth had surprised herself with the flow of lies she had told in such a short space of time.

So, Auntie Mildred needed to stay for at least a week. *Wait till I tell Jordan*. Beth wasn't looking forward to that.

In the car, Auntie Mildred started to laugh (she knew this was to be short-lived as she could already feel the pain in her head).

"What are you laughing at?" Beth had an idea though.

"Oh, you little minx. You knew you couldn't say you lived there and so as soon as you knew where she lived, I could see the scenarios spinning around your head."

"I think we need to get close to her, Auntie Mildred. We can ask all sorts of questions about the house and she won't have any idea why we care."

The drive home seemed really quick. *It's always the way*, she thought. They passed the bench that she had been laying on only hours before. The light was beginning to break through the pitch black of night.

They needed to go to bed and she hoped Jordan and Monty would already be in bed, but she could see as she pulled into the drive, that the light was on in the kitchen. Jordan, through habit, would have turned it off.

"Beth, look!"

Auntie Mildred had managed to get out of the car without help and was standing in front of the garage door. Beth, at that moment, was surprised it was closed and then she remembered it was a total lie about the door being left open in the first place.

In bright red paint (*How unimaginative*, thought Beth), someone had written:

> **If you want to stay alive
> go back to were you came from
> you old Witch**

"Whoever did this can't spell," Monty said, appearing from the kitchen. "It's '*where* you came from'. How uneducated. Anyway, how are you, Auntie?"

"I can't leave for a week," was her only response.

Jordan's head appeared from the kitchen door.

"What did they do, remove a leg?"

"When you think about it, I saw a shadow by the garage door. Whoever wrote that did so to scare you off. Why would they come back at that hour on the off chance you would be standing on the quietest road in England?"

They all agreed that this made no sense at all.

They went to bed – each one knowing that any sleep they were to have would be nominal.

When Auntie Mildred woke up, initially she had forgotten about her head until she realised she could only open one eye.

The pain was really bad. It wasn't very often she felt vulnerable but, right now, she really did. She didn't want to be on her own. She decided she would keep this to herself, but one thing was for sure, she was staying here until this thing played out to the end.

Two painkillers and the rest of the brandy from the bottle in her bag and she was back to sleep.

This was something the other three were glad about. Almost the same feeling new parents have when a newborn has a couple of hours on a warm, sunny Saturday afternoon.

Beth and Jordan were the only two downstairs. They were washing the garage door.

Initially, Jordan thought it needed a repaint, but realised it was kids' paint that washed off pretty easily, which was a bonus.

Monty, much to everyone's surprise, even his own, was drinking tea.

"I haven't slept a single bloody wink all night. We should really go to the police, but I know there is no point. There's no evidence of anything we saw that night, Beth, and all we have to go on is someone painted something on the garage door that you have now washed off. I don't suppose you took a photo before you scrubbed it?"

Both shook their heads in shame.

"No, I thought as much. Call yourself a sleuth, Beth? Then, we have an old lady who says she was smacked over the head while standing in the middle of the road in the early hours of the morning. No-one will believe us. I'm not even sure *I* believe us."

Everyone knew he was right.

There must be a way of cultivating some evidence from somewhere.

Beth relayed the events in the hospital. The girl from the Hall who was a nurse had actually offered her number so that she could help Auntie Mildred if need be.

"Well, this is progress indeed, Beth. So, tell us, Miss Marple, what is your plan?"

"Apparently, she lives in the Gate House with the housekeeper. I got the impression she didn't really enjoy the main house. I'm not too sure she gets on well with her family, but we didn't really have too much of a conversation about that. I was thinking though, I could befriend her; maybe go out for a drink with her. She thinks we are staying with our aunt and I said we'd stay until she was better, which is at least a week. Shall I call her to see if she'd like to go to the pub one night and maybe I could find out a little more?"

Deciding there was nothing to be lost in her doing so, Beth made the call. She and Flora made a date for the following evening.

Jordan received a call, which he took outside. He didn't look too happy afterwards.

"Who pissed on your chips?" Monty asked him.

"I need to go to Oz, to the mine. They think they have found a really deep silver ore. Apparently, it's huge and Rex thinks I need to be there."

This was not good timing at all.

For Beth, Jordan was her rock and leaving her in the middle of all of this was going to be difficult.

For Jordan, he felt he needed to stay home. His wife, after all, was his most precious jewel. He loved her more than anything in the world. He would offer her his brother to come and stay. Jordan knew he would be away for at least a month and Ben was pretty formidable.

"Absolutely, you must go," lied Beth. "Jordan, this is our retirement fund. You *have* to go. Definitely. Oh, and it's a no to Ben."

Ben, in Beth's eyes, was a spoiled brat. His parents had thought they'd only have one child, but nature had a different plan and along came Ben. He was much younger than Jordan. He was athletic, rugged and very good-looking (the opinion of the girls he courted), but he was also slightly arrogant and self-centred. The kind of son who ran home to his mummy and daddy with his dirty washing to camp out there for a week, take a chunk of money and then leave, not to be seen for months. He would try to humiliate

Jordan whenever he could, so both Beth and Jordan kept out of his way. Beth did, however, understand why he would be a good guard dog right now.

Looking at Monty, a man who was the least likely defence barrier, she could understand Jordan's rationale. Then Auntie Mildred, although she had a sharp tongue and was the only old lady Beth knew who rode a motorbike (with a name), she now had a frailty about her that she realised meant she could not be anywhere near these events.

Suddenly, Beth became a little excited by the idea that she was in the middle of all of this.

She knew what she had seen that night; she knew that man was dead.

Now, she needed to find the body or, at the very least, some kind of evidence. This is what she had dreamed of since she was a little girl. Yes, those dreams involved ghosts and some wrinkly guy at the end of the dream saying, 'I'd have gotten away with it if it hadn't been for those pesky kids', but all the same, she knew she would at some point in her life, be kneedeep in danger, but she hadn't reckoned on being neck deep in it.

Jordan was reluctantly making plans to fly to Oz. Beth had promised that she wouldn't put herself or anyone else in harm's way, at least until he got home. He'd said she could go out with Flora, but nothing more.

Since there was no body and no mention on the news either regional or national about anyone being hurt or having gone missing, it was highly probable that there had been a fight which led to someone getting hurt, but nothing more than that (or at least that's what they were all trying to convince each other had happened). The events, Jordan had convinced himself, had been warnings from a family who wanted to be left alone. *If someone goes to these lengths to warn you off in large painted letters, they are making themselves quite clear,* he thought. Extreme though their warnings had been, he had satisfied himself that he could go, Beth on a tight rein and the Monty and Auntie Mildred combo in situ to keep an eye on her.

Jordan knew that if he asked Monty to make sure Beth behaved herself, he need only make one call to determine if that was the case. Monty was useless at telling lies.

He would drive himself to the airport. This way, there needn't be a drama in the morning.

Monty, bless him (now on his first G&T of the day) was beside himself. He wasn't used to this. He had plans this week – lunches and cocktails, for God's sake – he had a life too. Bloody Beth and her adventures. He hadn't minded the ghost hunts. They had always had fun together. Saw nothing but ended up having such a laugh that he was always ready for their next expedition.

Now, here he was, with an injured aunt who drove him mad and a friend who potentially would have them all murdered in their sleep. Where was the guard dog? Did people hire dogs like that? He'd certainly feel happier with a growling, salivating beast pacing round the house at night. Then he remembered she was already there!

Beth, with her newfound confidence and also her night out with Flora the following evening, decided that she would call the dentist to have the check-up she had promised herself (Jordan would have to wait until he was back home. He had strong teeth anyway). Quietly, Beth had wanted to mix with the locals so that she could sound them out. OK, this wasn't what Jordan had written on his list of dos and don'ts, but teeth are important, so she made the call and got herself booked in for that Friday (two days away).

Auntie Mildred walked into the kitchen.

"My head hurts like a bitch."

They all turned round to see the full extent of what had happened to this poor old lady the night before.

"I have never meant this more in my life than I do right now, but fucking hell, Auntie Mildred! Beth, take a photo of her face right now."

"Beth, don't you bloody dare?" came the reply from what were now swollen, purple lips.

Beth took a photo, which, in her eyes, made up for her foolishly not having taken a photo of the garage door.

They spent the day doing nothing. Not even really speaking to one another. Jordan was busy packing – he never really took much with him, preferring to travel light (unless he was going away with Beth, which was a different thing altogether).

Auntie Mildred lay on the sofa. The tablets and brandy seemed to sedate her, so Monty made sure that her bottle and glass were frequently filled. He wasn't too sure if that was medically OK, but today he needed some space in his head to sort out what he thought he should do.

After all, from tomorrow he would be the man of the house.

Beth had a bath, shaved her legs, reapplied her nail varnish to her toes (fingers were gels, so they were OK), gave herself a St Tropez tan and then did her hair. Jordan would think it was for his benefit, but deep down she knew she would be unlikely to have the time to do these things with all of the other plans she had mapped out in order to solve this crime (she had decided in the bath that it was her duty to solve this).

Dinner was a simple event; liquids only for Mildred while the others had smoked salmon and scrambled eggs. Beth wasn't a great cook, hence the disaster steak pie earlier, but she was delighted in telling everyone she could do most things with an egg. Wine, thankfully, goes with most things, so this kept the conversation going until Jordan signed off for the night. He needed to get up early to catch his flight.

"Don't you think you should go up with him, Beth?" asked Monty. This would give him time to watch his programmes on TV – escapism, if you will.

"No way, Monty. He'll be asleep already and if I read my book, I disturb him so no, let's have a glass of Baileys and play Scrabble."

"Darling, Beth, that is the drink of the devil. It will strip your insides. Really, it's full of shit."

"Darling, Monty, I wouldn't worry about *your* insides, they are long gone and mine seem to relax as its silky velvet qualities comfort my digestive tract."

They both chuckled at that and, for a moment, seemed to forget about recent events.

A few games of Scrabble later and fouler language than anyone should ever have to hear, they heard the wailing of what they thought was a cow in calf.

"Crap, it's Auntie Mildred."

They had been drinking Baileys and were both very drunk. It seemed to take them away from the things they didn't want to either think or talk about.

Reality soon came flooding back.

"Anyone? I need help!"

Sober in seconds, they both ran upstairs, almost racing one another.

Auntie Mildred was in the bathroom. She had decided to have a shower, but couldn't get the top she was wearing and which she had decided to pull down, all the way, and it hurt just as much when attempting to take it off over her head.

This was a sight that Monty certainly didn't wish to see ever again.

Clearly, this garment was the first thing she tried to put on. Nothing was hidden other than her face, which was probably a good thing considering she didn't see him almost gagging. He promptly turned and left the room leaving Beth to deal with the problem.

The top had to be cut almost in half.

Just when she was ready for bed (with Monty safely exited – smiling as he went, knowing Mildred would keep Beth up for hours), Mildred had asked Beth to join her for a drink. Beth chose black coffee.

Beth wanted to ask Mildred how old she actually was (she had always played a game with herself where she would try to guess people's ages. Very boring game now, she came to think about it). Whilst dressed and made up to the nines, as she usually was, the sight just now was also one she didn't want to see again either. She did find herself looking at Auntie Mildred and thought to herself how well she looked when she was dressed. Clothes are very important she decided, as was make-up and well styled hair – at any age, it would seem.

After an hour of small talk, they both went to bed.

Everyone was asleep in minutes. No-one at that point really cared or even thought about what could be going on outside.

CHAPTER SEVEN

Waterdale Hall, to most on the outside looking in, would see splendour and imagine themselves living there. The high life, the glamour and the fun.

The reality was, however, something quite different.

Lady Grey found her solace in the garden. It seemed to be the only place her husband never wished to be found.

Over the years, they seemed to have found solace in their own individual worlds, hers being the garden and his, more so nowadays, his study from where he never seemed to be off the phone. That was, of course, when he was at home. More frequently nowadays, he found many reasons to go to London, reasons she didn't question because, deep down, she didn't really care. His absences gave her the calm and solitude she craved. He generally made life quite tense and the staff sensed this too.

One day last week, Lady Grey swore she had heard him arguing in such a way she had tried to balance herself on a large stone in one of the borders – that was until Frank, the gardener, thought she had caught her skirt on a rose bush and came to help her out. She could hardly confess that she had been ear-wigging, so had to allow him to help her out from the various plants… and so the intrigue continued.

The house, finally, had been finished internally. Every room had been lovingly decorated and restored back to its former glory. Tasteful, yet with much more light than its darker days. It had been her choosing. For years, she was sick of the wooden panelling her husband seemed so fascinated with, so other than the genuine Jacobean wood panels, she had removed the false panelling and decorated to her taste. Strangely enough, he didn't seem to care that he'd had no input at all. She had been pleased about his lack of interest; it had meant she could go out with Flora and sometimes Agnes too and they would walk around the shops and discuss colour and fabrics.

On one occasion, the three of them went to London and found a lovely little Italian restaurant near Harrods. They had lunch and wine. Lady Grey remembers laughing an awful lot. She missed that – laughter. Her husband had made sure her only friends were mutual friends; she was quite sad she didn't have anyone close that she could just sit in the snug and have coffee with and laugh about stupid things on TV or something that had happened. It was because nothing ever happened any more in her life that she laughed so little. In some ways, she was angry with herself for allowing things to have become so bad. It was obvious they no longer loved one another, but a divorce would cause so much pain to the children. This, of course, was only something she assumed. What child *didn't* love their father or mother for that matter? Especially a child who had been born into such a privileged life?

This, she decided, was another sign that her husband was slowly detaching himself from her and this beautiful house. Their children were older and would soon, she guessed, want to leave to start their own lives elsewhere. Whilst this saddened her, she felt she didn't really know her children as well as she should. She had never wanted them to board. Children should be at home, she felt, when they are very young. Later on, if it had been their choice to board, then that was OK, but not so young. Her relationship with her daughter was a special one, but really, they should spend more time talking and doing things together. Lady Grey decided that she would make sure this happened sooner rather than later.

When she had spoken with both Flora and Felix, neither of them seemed to want to follow tradition and take up the family seat. She guessed she would end her days living with Agnes in the main house and they could both keep each other company.

Agnes was her friend; they had many things in common but nothing more so than their mutual lack of love for Lord Grey. Lady

Grey had given up on that ghost long ago and Agnes had never seemed to care for him. He was very rude and didn't seem to want to hide that from anyone who visited – unless of course, you were thirty-something and very attractive.

Flora loathed her father. She knew that was very odd; after all, he did contribute to giving her life, but she chose not to believe that, in fact, she was actually hopeful that her mother had once had an affair with a loving, kind chap. Choosing to believe this seemed to make it easier hating her greedy, arrogant, lazy father. Flora knew that her father wanted only one thing, which was access to the family fund. Her mother was worth hundreds of millions of pounds and her father made no secret in the fact that he would fight tooth and nail if she ever asked him to leave, for what he thought was his 50% right to her particular pot of gold.

Flora respected her mother who had worked very hard her whole life to maintain this house and surrounding land. They had many people on the payroll, but very few who were allowed to get close to the family. This had actually been her grandmother's wish and that ideal had been passed down to her mother and then down to her. Her grandmother was a ratty old cow. Flora had no time for her. She had been a raging snob and Flora didn't like that. Her own mother, meanwhile, thankfully believed that people didn't work *for* her, rather they worked *with* her and most of the staff loved her for that.

Agnes, who Flora adored, lived in the Gate House. Frank, the gardener, had moved in with her only a year ago. His family were all over the place, brothers and sisters from various fathers, some known, some not. Frank had no idea who his father was, but he knew that he had been very lucky to find this job and that was thanks to Agnes and her late husband. He had known nothing about plants and gardening in general until he started to work here. Now, since Agnes' husband's death, the family had offered him his old job, which was to make sure all the staff were doing the things they were supposed to do. At only 22, he took great pride in what he did. Everyone liked him.

It was actually Flora who Frank liked the most. They were

similar in age and he felt quite protective towards her. When she qualified as a nurse, it was he, Agnes and her mother who had acknowledged her great achievement. They had each bought her a gift; he had bought her a fob watch (he'd asked another nurse what he could buy her). Flora loved it and wore it every day for work. To Frank, this gesture seemed to bind them together. He loved her, but she had no idea. He had once almost told her and then decided not to – he knew this could potentially ruin their friendship and also cost him his job.

Agnes knew all about Frank and his feelings for Flora; he would confide in her. Agnes had thought it best, given their young age, to keep things as they were and then see if and how things changed over the years to come.

Flora and Agnes always talked about matters of the heart. Agnes had a great sense of humour, which was lost living within this family, Flora would tell her. Agnes realised that she had hardly ever seen any of them smile let alone laugh. Money does not buy happiness. Agnes and her husband had very little, but they had a very deep love for one another and they chuckled all the time. What was the point of all this glamour and grandeur when you appeared to be void of all emotion?

Agnes treasured her relationship with Flora; she was the daughter she had never been blessed with and, Frank, the son her husband had longed for. It wasn't to be for them.

Felix, Flora's brother, shared far too many similarities to his father. He was rude – Agnes knew when she was in his company that she was staff and not family. His father made her feel the same way. Felix was entitled; he didn't work (why should he? His family were loaded). His attitude was such that he was always to have the best, noisiest car; he would travel to London to see his old school friends (who actually did work). He was also a playboy. Agnes didn't think he had ever been in the Gate House. What reason could there be to lure him in to the smallest house on the estate? None, in fact. For that, Agnes was thankful.

Felix did, however, stay on the right side of his father. He knew that his daddy would always cough up when asked – he didn't even need to provide reasons for wanting cash. It was on tap. Both he and his father shared that lust. Mummy, however, was not a cash machine; it was always very difficult getting money out of her. When he talked about his mother to his friends, he would call her 'a tight bitch'. His friends didn't share this opinion; they all thought his mother was lovely. They didn't care for his father too much though. Felix would see his friendship group dwindle if he continued with this kind of lifestyle. His friends were all genuinely decent young men. Their girlfriends were equally as nice. When they had visited the Hall, they were always apologetic that they'd arrived clearly without prior agreement by Lady Grey who always liked to have things arranged. That was the only thing she was quite specific about. She liked to have the things in that their guests liked to eat and drink. For Felix, he didn't worry about such things. Drugs did play a part in this – socially at first, but this became much more frequent as time went on. At some point, the friends who didn't partake would no longer be there for him. This seemed to be pretty much all of them. Over time, he brought other friends round. They had not been the types of people his mother liked at all. The boys were loud and drank too much (and smoked anything) and the girls dressed like hookers. Flora had once said they were actually hookers, a fact Felix was proud to admit. "Why go for a boring girl who hangs on to you for your money when you can pay for a real beauty?"

"Isn't that the same thing?" Flora had asked him.

Felix couldn't see it.

The relationship between Flora and Felix barely existed. The house was so big that they could avoid each other quite easily. This suited them both – until, of course, there was a dinner, then they were forced into polite conversation. This was how they had been educated and Flora hated it because it was false. It was for this very reason she chose to spend so much time with Agnes and Frank (who she loved to spend time with. He made her laugh out loud and she loved to laugh).

Beth was getting herself ready for her evening with Flora in the 'Gateway to Hell' as Monty called it.

Monty was sitting on her bed, which irritated Beth just a little bit – Jordan had left and she felt quite upset about that and thought she might have a bit of a cry before she got ready, but Monty had put paid to that.

He felt he needed to talk her through the 'what to say' and the 'what not to say' scenarios.

"You have to remember that you don't live here; you're staying with your aunt who has injured herself, which Flora knows – we are three friends. When the truth is out, Beth, everyone will understand your web of lies."

"I know that and I'm quite good at keeping to the story, Monty. I am, after all, the sleuth here."

Monty gave her a sideways look and reminded her that it wasn't particularly sleuth-like when she had washed vital evidence from the garage door.

Point taken, she thought.

"What shall I wear?"

"Beth, it's not a date. Wear a pair of jeans and go casual."

It still took her 40 minutes to decide what she'd put on. Her rationale was that she couldn't remember if they were staying at the Gate House or going to the pub. She hoped the former – that way there was little chance of busybody questions.

Beth made her way to the Gate House. She had walked, which was something she loved to do. Flora was Beth's cup of tea. Kind, thoughtful and actually quite good fun, she remembered, from their meeting at the hospital. Tonight should be a fun evening, *but don't forget the purpose of being here*, she reminded herself.

What a lovely girl, thought Agnes. *Shame she doesn't live more local.* Although she had no idea what they were talking about, Agnes found herself giggling along with them.

They were actually laughing at Auntie Mildred.

"She actually rides a motorbike and has given it a name. In fairness, she's lucky her only injuries were with the garage door."

"Is she confident on the roads?" Flora asked, still chuckling.

"I think she has almost no regard for anyone else on the road. She should drive with some kind of alert to other motorists." Beth hadn't, in fact, ever seen Mildred on the road, but Monty had given her enough detail over the years.

"Let's stay here, I can't be bothered to go to the house to get changed," said Flora who was still in her tracksuit. All of her dressy clothes were in her bedroom in the main house.

Agnes was already on the case and had asked both of them what they wanted to drink. Beth needed to stay focused and so asked for lemonade. Flora had green tea.

"What a pair of lightweights!" Agnes laughed.

Flora talked about her childhood. Beth decided to start young and establish the mechanics behind the family.

It didn't take too long to work out everything she needed to know about their sad and boring lives. Holidays were literally them just being home from boarding school. Parents too wrapped up in themselves to do anything with them.

That was when the strong bond between Flora and Agnes was born. Agnes used to teach Flora how to cook, clean and take care of the home, explaining to her the importance of looking after her own house when she had one.

Agnes supposed that this was one of the reasons Flora went into nursing – she liked to take care of people and things in general.

Flora's father did not like the fact his daughter had a job. Flora had explained to him that she felt it was her calling. He just couldn't get his head around why she felt she needed to work.

"But I *want* to, Father."

"Whoever *wants* to, Flora?" Your time could be better spent here. Your mother could do with some help with the house."

"No, I couldn't," Lady Grey replied – and that was the end of that.

Beth asked about the history to the house and the Ghost (she also explained that she was an avid ghost hunter).

Flora was fascinated by this and told Beth about the maze of tunnels under the house/grounds and various parts of the village dating way back to when kings used to use the tunnels to travel around unnoticed.

Now Beth was sitting up.

"Tunnels, wow! Do you go down there ever? Does *any*one go down there?"

"Me, never. My brother was far more adventurous when he was younger. I seem to remember him getting lost at one point. It was Agnes' husband who found him. I think he found an old map dating back hundreds of years." Flora was happy to talk about the old days. Beth was more than happy to listen.

A map, thought Beth. *I need that map.*

"So, did you send the map to a museum or anything? They love things like that."

"No, my mother has it framed in the drawing room. I must admit, it's quite an interesting thing to look at. Would you like to see it?"

Just as Beth was about to say yes, she thought better of it. What if anyone living in the house or one of the groundsmen was in the room that night and recognised her? No, she would wait and speak with Monty first.

Beth felt sorry that Flora had had such a lonely upbringing, comparing it to her own, which was filled with love and the joys of life.

The only other thing that Beth gleaned from their conversation was the night the incident happened – there had been the huge party. Beth had forgotten about that.

Her mind was whizzing around with all sorts of possibilities.

Then, all of a sudden, from nowhere, Flora told Beth that there was a tunnel, the starting point of which was to the left of the back door at the Gate House.

"Oh wow, how cool is that? Who else knows it's there?" Beth had to act as casual as she could. Right now, all she could think about was the starting point to a new adventure. The web of tunnels could uncover whatever it is they needed to find to solve the mystery of the night of the incident.

"No idea," replied Flora. It was clear they didn't share the excitement Beth had about this matrix of mystery.

OK, thought Beth, *enough of the investigative questioning. Let's get the hilarity back.* She had cultivated enough info for one evening. She had to now plan the next move she and Monty would be making.

They cracked up about all sorts of things. Agnes was a real hoot, too. Beth had them in snorting fits about Auntie Mildred. They all laughed some more about her relationship with Monty and how they met.

Agnes told them all about her childhood (she seemed to be as fortunate as Beth had been growing up).

Walking home, in the dark, Beth suddenly felt very vulnerable. It had never occurred to her that the dark could play horrible tricks with the mind. Her resolve was that if she couldn't be seen, then no-one should be able to see her.

That hadn't helped Auntie Mildred the other night.

Once safely home, she was very surprised that both Monty and Auntie Mildred were in bed.

Phew.

Beth was more than happy to fall into bed to hopefully catch up on the sleep she had missed out on over the last couple of nights.

Finding herself a little jealous that Jordan could sleep on a clothesline and would probably have 23 hours of slumber all the way to Oz, she was asleep before she even had the chance to give it any more thought.

"What the bloody hell was that?" shouted Monty.

Beth was now awake. Looking at the clock she realised, just before she began to rant about her lack of sleep, she'd been in bed for nine hours.

Eight am. Monty was awake. He'd actually been awake for over an hour. Drinking coffee – he'd figured he would need as much caffeine as possible to get through Beth's tales of the night before.

He could see Auntie Mildred's bike on the drive. Good old Betsy.

On his second, more focused look, he could see something sitting on the seat. Whatever it was didn't look very happy. He'd go outside to get a better look.

Sitting along the seat, paws up on the handlebars (as far as they could reach) was a black cat.

A dead, black cat.

That's when Auntie Mildred and Beth heard Monty shout out.

There was no blood.

Beth, looking through the window, saw the cat. She ran downstairs as fast as she could.

Auntie Mildred went into the bathroom for a shower. Whatever had caused Monty to shout out could wait until she was ready.

"Who the hell put that there?" Monty circled the bike with roughly a metre gap as he did the round trip.

"Monty, this is another warning. Look at the note pinned to the number plate at the back."

"Here's your cat, you old witch," he read out. "You'll be next if you don't leave."

This time, Beth took a photo.

The cat was stuffed.

"This isn't a hardened criminal, Monty, they would use a real cat."

"That's as hardened as anyone needs to be, in my opinion. I think we should go to the flat in London until things calm down, or at least until Jordan gets back."

"We can't Monty, we have something we need to do tomorrow night."

"And what might that be?"

"We have to find our way back to that room."

"No chance. You promised Jordan and I promised him I'd look after you."

"That's what you'll be doing. Oh, and I have the dentist this afternoon."

Auntie Mildred, freshly washed, hair in a bun and glass in her hand, appeared at the door at half ten.

"Where's the fire, Monty?" This was always her first question following one of his dramatic outpourings.

"No fire, Auntie, just a dead cat and another threat."

"Right, let's take a look."

With that, she was off to the garage to see what the fuss was about.

"This is schoolyard stuff, Monty. No-one sends a stuffed cat thinking they're frightening someone. 'Go or you're next', what are they going to do, stuff me?"

"Put it in the bin and forget about it."

Beth hated the dentist but she hated toothache even more. Today, though, the visit was less about teeth and more about information.

The dentist, quite a smart chap. Middle-aged and seemingly of good humour. Once they had worked around her mouth and established she needed to continue flossing and brushing in a circular motion twice a day, he began to chat about her move and the goings-on in the village.

"It's a busy little place, actually," the dentist began. "Lots of gossip – usually of who knew of a missing dog or 'Watch out for the rabbit holes along the footpath', but then the other day I saw a chap with three teeth missing. What a job that was. He'd been punched in the face. Cost him a fortune. He had no clue who did it, so just watch out if you're out walking. Do you have a dog? He's coming back for a follow-up; he's in after you, actually."

Holy crap! How would she get out of that?

"If you could pay downstairs," said the rather refreshingly friendly dental nurse, with a smile.

"Where's the loo?" asked Beth, who didn't need to go at all. What she needed was a diversion.

As she dived in to the loo, she could hear the dental nurse walking up the stairs with the chap Beth felt sure was the man who attacked Auntie Mildred.

She had barely opened the door but, as she looked behind, it was enough to catch sight of a very tall man. From behind he looked older than she had expected. Jet-black hair and very, very well dressed.

In her haste, she almost forgot to pay for her check-up.

The receptionist was quick to remind her.

"You didn't think to wait until he came out then, Beth the super sleuth?"

Monty was right. Missed opportunity.

She was so keen to get home to report back, she hadn't thought of that. Note for next time.

CHAPTER EIGHT

"So," said Monty, "the upside to us doing this is there isn't one."

Monty paced the floor – he liked to do this when he was having a Sherlock moment.

Beth knew the drill.

"The downside, however, is a seemingly longer list:-

The last time we did anything like this, we think we saw someone die…

… terrible expletives were painted onto the garage door…

…Auntie Mildred had a hit on her and then she was in fact, attacked…

…more expletives and an already dead cat sitting on her motorcycle.

"I'm not saying that I am going back there this evening willingly. With our usual adventures I often do, but this particular adventure, in the knowledge the chap who is the most likely candidate for Auntie Mildred's whack is, as you describe, a goliath of a chap – I'm looking forward to this even less."

Beth took to her feet.

"Get your coat, Monty, we're off."

Auntie Mildred gave him her cosh, which, Beth noticed, he took without a moment's hesitation.

Leaving everything until after midnight has its advantages, thought Beth. *The disadvantages would be an afterthought.*

The back door opened, shedding light across the drive – revealing them creeping across the drive.

"Be careful," said Auntie Mildred. Thankfully, her eye, lip and various bruises seemed less feisty (thanks to Bio-Oil) – not actually a tip from Flora, but one from Beth's mother who swore by it.

This simple statement seemed to emphasise the potential danger they were putting themselves in.

Beth had decided she wouldn't give Monty too much information before they left – he asked far too many sensible questions that she couldn't answer. They walked very hesitantly across the road and through the gap in the hedge. It was Beth this time who had the encounter with the boulder. Monty, slightly smug, crawled through with ease.

They sat in the middle of the trees so that Beth could debrief him.

They were to go back to the room. There had to be something there. They couldn't, however, go back down the same set of steps. This was too much of a risk. They would use the tunnel from the Gate House. Monty referenced the mining torch Jordan had used which minimised reflective light. From her pockets, Beth revealed two not identical, but very similar torches she had found in Jordan's cupboard. Having already tested them, she handed one to Monty. They stood up and walked as cautiously and stealthily as they could to the Gate House. Inside, Beth could see everyone had gone to bed. Agnes didn't believe in closing the curtains.

"Days are short enough," she had said that night. "Anyway, who can see *in* here?"

Beth had no clue if or how the door to the tunnel opened. All she knew was that it was situated to the side of the back door.

It was actually Monty who both found and opened the door. It had been sitting beneath a plant pot full of smaller plant pots. If you didn't know it was there, you would never have known. It wasn't so much covered, but it looked to be part of the patio and a small ivy bush had grown around it and slightly over one corner. As it opened, Beth shone her torch inside and, this time, the steps were much more user-friendly. They were made of stone and not steep at all. What she couldn't see was the actual depth.

They looked at each other and nothing was said.

Beth knew both Frank and Agnes had rooms overlooking the front of the house, so she had decided they should leave the door open, just in case anything terrible happened whilst they were down there and needed to rush back.

It was Beth (as always) who took the first steps down. They had to go down backwards to hold on to the steps – no rails down here and, unfortunately, no way of seeing where they were heading, other than down. Monty followed her – twice stepping on her fingers. She didn't cry out and he didn't apologise.

The steps Beth counted, totalled 33. On went her torch. On went Monty's torch.

Shining it around wherever they were, they realised that the downside of these torches was that they really did minimise their level of vision. Beth had left her phone at home as had Monty, however, not knowing Beth would have these with her, he brought the torch his Auntie Mildred had in her bag – it was a dumpy little thing, but actually quite bright and, down here, it was a welcome addition.

They were not in a room; it was more like the next level. There had to be either a door or more stairs. As Monty continued to shine the torch, they saw more stairs in the far corner. These were less kind – metal of some kind but very old and rusty. There were only 11 of these.

As they made their way down the steps, both of them made reference to the pungent smell.

"Beth, really, where the hell are we heading? Do you have a plan from here because I am not seeing any door, trap or otherwise. There is a smell in here that, not to put too fine a point on it, fucking stinks!"

Beth couldn't argue with him. This seemed to be a dead end. The smell, she concurred, *was* vile.

"OK, Monty, no actual plan from here, I thought it would just be another route to the room we were under. Logic though, suggests that there should be some way forward, otherwise what was the point of digging this tunnel?"

"There is a way forward, Beth, it's called turning around and going back up those stairs."

As he walked across the floor, they both heard the change in the sound of his feet on the ground. He had walked over something wooden. That had to be the door they were looking for.

It was Monty who bent down to see how it could open. As he reached down, they both heard voices. The voices were below them and were clearly walking right beneath their own feet. Once again, neither of them moved or said a word. The voices were two males however and, once again, the voices were muffled, but when they did hear them with more clarity, they were raised voices. Monty, who lay flat on the floor, ear pressed to the wooden door, had the best chance of piecing the sentences together.

Beth stood stone still and waited for some kind of update.

His torch off, the mining torch on but facing one of the walls, they stared at each other. Beth frowned in an attempt to understand what Monty could hear.

More raised voices and then Monty slowly raised himself from the floor. His hair was full of dust and sticking out all over the place on the side he lay on. His lime cashmere was also full of dust – *Another casualty*, thought Beth. Monty, she noticed as he came closer to her, wide-eyed, was walking as they do in war-torn countries, as if trying to avoid an Improvised Explosive Device.

He didn't appear to want to speak. Beth gestured towards the steps. He scaled them effortlessly. Beth was right behind him.

On the next level, Monty, again in the lead, began his ascent. Beth started to feel scared for the first time. Surely the men wouldn't be coming up to where they were. If so many people knew about the tunnel, Agnes would have mentioned this and, also, the door didn't look like it had been opened in years, possibly tens of years.

Thankful that she had left the door open, they found themselves in the dense darkness of night. Happy to be there. Still on mute, they retraced their steps back to the house.

Once inside, they sat at the table and it was Beth who poured them both a very large glass of wine.

"What just happened?" Beth asked. She'd been there, she'd organised the whole thing and now, she looked at her friend who looked like he'd seen the ghost they had originally planned to see on that very first visit, covered in crap, and it was all her doing. He was doing this for her.

"Monty, wait." Beth stood up and walked over to him. Bending down, Monty pulled his head away.

"Surely you're not going to kiss me, are you?"

"What? No. I'd laugh at that normally, Monty; I'm looking at your head. I think you may have cut your head open."

"Cut my head? On what?" Monty touched his head. He was certain he had no wound on his head.

Beth grabbed some kitchen roll, wet it and began to wipe his hair, but she stopped suddenly in her tracks.

"Monty, this isn't your blood."

"What are you saying, Beth?"

"We need to go back down there. I think the blood belongs to our missing dead person."

"What did you hear, Monty?"

"They were talking about moving it."

"The body?"

"I don't know, I couldn't hear everything, but they were definitely talking about moving it. Beth, we can't go back down there. Think about it; if the blood was on our level, that means they moved it from the top down. They could be using that as access."

Beth got one of the plastic pots she used for her salad dressings, grabbed a pair of scissors and then, with one swift clip, cut off rather more of Monty's blood-soaked hair than she had intended, which she immediately put into her sealed container. Pen in hand, she marked the lid detailing what was inside.

Monty, jumping straight up, looked at himself in the mirror.

"You absolute bitch! You callous, clumsy bitch! Look at the state of me, Beth."

Beth had to admit it was a real chunk and tried to brush his longer strands over the gap.

"I'm going for a shower. Don't go to bed, I'm coming right back down."

Beth had no intention of going to bed. There was only one place she was going.

The climb down seemed much quicker. This time, she took

her phone and only her phone. She needed to see if the trap door opened. Certain that it would, she cleared an area around the edge and found that it would lift pretty easily. The coast was clear apart from what looked like a dustbin in the corner of the room (there were four doors leading off this room).

Trying to lift the lid, she realised it wouldn't budge. The smell coming from whatever was inside was really awful.

She took a photo of the bin.

Then, as quickly as she had found her way down, she made her way back up.

As she walked across the gravel, it was no surprise that Monty was waiting for her.

"I know where you've been. This has now gone too far. I'm calling the police."

"No, Monty, let me show you what I found. If we have to, we'll call them in the morning."

Monty looked at the bin.

"That doesn't prove anything, Beth."

"Exactly. We need more."

The next morning they got just that.

Auntie Mildred was first up.

Feeling sore, but happy that she'd had a decent quota of sleep, she found herself doing something she rarely did – she was washing-up.

Beth was next up and was delighted to see a very clean kitchen. Even happier when she was offered a cup of tea.

The two of them sat in the kitchen trying to make sense of what they were in the middle of.

"I'm going to tell you something, Beth, I have had a very varied life. Lots of things have happened to me, some good, some not so good. I've had adventures of sorts, but nothing remotely compares to this. It's scary, I shan't lie, but I feel as though I'm in the middle of something that really matters and I am looking forward to helping you solve this mystery."

Beth relayed the events of the night before.

Both women agreed that the bin could be anything, something

or nothing.

"You need to make yourself busy in that house, Beth. You need to work your friendship with the daughter and get in. The husband would be my first choice or the son."

Monty made his way into the kitchen. He'd been up a while, but he had taken extra time on his hair. This proved pointless; he would just have to let it grow out.

Auntie Mildred stared at him long and hard. Anything she wanted to say to him, she felt would have to wait. The worry etched on his face was enough for her to park any remarks until later.

Beth, who just couldn't get away from that smell, was carrying the bin liner outside. Anything remotely stinky had to go.

As she opened the door, she stopped dead in her tracks. Sitting in the middle of the drive was the dustbin that she had seen deep below the earth's surface last night.

How did anyone know she had seen it?

Who could possibly have seen her?

Now, most importantly, what the hell would they find inside it?

Monty followed her out with his squashed tea bags.

"OK, let's get on and open it then. Put your bag in your bin and let's see what we've been sent this time."

CHAPTER NINE

Jordan had this niggling feeling that he just couldn't seem to shift.

His wife, although quite brave on the outside and very adventurous naturally, did, very often, dive right into situations without any regard for any potential fear involved.

Monty, lovely though he is, is no defence mechanism in any situation. Auntie Mildred would be a safer bet.

Looking at his watch, then deciding she would probably be in bed, thought he'd give her another couple of hours and then call her.

The work on the mine was far more involved than he'd anticipated. The drilling had been so successful that word had travelled fast around the markets. Investors were now calling his office to question amounts, etc, obviously keen to be the first to hit the market headlines and buy in at the lowest price prior to lift-off.

He was tired and didn't fancy eating with the others. He just wanted to go back to the hotel, grab a cold beer and eat something light, probably while watching some king of Aussie soap that he usually expected to hate, but found himself getting drawn into watching every night.

Once in his room, he sat, beer in hand, and smiled to himself as he thought about Beth.

'The love of his life' he had called her during his wedding speech. And she was. Fun, loving, caring and always there for him. She was his rock and he was hers. He knew there was no price he could ever put on their relationship. He would, quite literally, die for her.

His phone suddenly kicked into life – or had he fallen asleep?

The latter, he decided. Beer bottle still in his hand and quite full – that wouldn't be the case if he'd been awake.

And there it was, a text from Beth.

Hey lovely you !!

Don't be mad but this could be quite bad and I wanted to speak with you before we did anything because I don't want to make matters any worse than they are.

They are already very, very bad.

There wasn't really time for him to be angry or think about emotion of any kind. Beth had written to say that she had been into another tunnel and found the bin, which was now sitting on their driveway.

we haven't dared to open it yet – it really stinks Jordan she had put in her text.

She wanted him to video call her so that they could see each other.

And call her he did.

Beth was sure she hadn't felt this nervous since her wedding day.

The promise she had made to Jordan had been broken and she had broken it knowing that he would be angry with her, but her own sheer bloody-mindedness forced her to do it. That's what Beth did, her own thing. Anyone who gave her advice, she would listen to it. She always knew, with Jordan, that his was the right advice, but when it came to her sleuthing, she always felt that needed to take charge.

The advice she gave to herself, she felt, right now, was not always the right advice.

Here was the call. She had taken herself to their room – not wanting either Monty or Auntie Mildred to hear her telling off (rightly so, they would both have concluded).

No, she had to face this particular piece of music alone.

"Hey," she tried to sound casually loving.

"Hey." Jordan's tone was loving, but full of concern.

"What the hell, Beth!"

"I really wanted to prove to everyone what we saw that night. I actually thought I'd cracked it – taken a photo to show to Monty–"

"Wait, you went down there on your own? What the bloody hell were you thinking, Beth? Jee-zus."

Beth explained about the blood, Monty's hair…

"OK, let's go outside and take a look. I'm telling you, Beth, if that's a body…" he started, before bursting into sudden laughter.

"Listen to me, 'if that's a body…', like it's a normal thing for us to be talking about!"

He's so hot! thought Beth as she made her way down the stairs, knowing that this was not the appropriate time to lust after her husband.

Monty and Auntie Mildred were sitting at the table, both pretending to be locked in conversation, but the reality was that they'd been listening, waiting for the fireworks.

"Auntie Mildred, you stay in the house." This was Jordan's insistence. "If this is something sinister, I don't want you to see it."

Auntie Mildred seemed to take his instruction rather well. Much as she busybodies her way through her life, the whack she had the other night was a shock to her system. The fact that she seemed to be the one they were targeting, she thought it best to stay away.

One thought that *did* cross her mind was that if they thought *she* was the snoop, surely they didn't think she was lithe and agile enough to find her way down the tunnel. Perhaps she didn't give herself enough credit. Clearly, she appeared to be more athletic-looking than she had thought – either that or they thought she must be quite able-bodied to be riding a motorcycle.

Beth appeared with Monty, who was wearing an airtight face covering and had sprayed himself with the air freshener Beth kept by the back door.

Under normal circumstances, she could have accused him of

smelling worse than the bin, but not today. This was very serious.

"Do you both have gloves on?"

Monty did.

Beth did not, so it would be Monty who would take the lid off the bin.

It was a struggle. "It's too tight. It isn't moving."

Beth handed the phone to Monty. "Give me the gloves." Completely without any reluctance whatsoever, Monty peeled them off and handed them to Beth.

Managing to twist the lid, she knew that the next twist would see the lid removed from the bin itself.

Looking up at Monty and hearing Jordan asking him to reverse the camera so that he could see immediately what was inside, Beth removed the lid. She wasn't looking inside.

"What's that?" Jordan was asking. "Move closer, Monty."

Beth turned to look inside the bin.

It was full to the brim with fish guts and maggots.

"Another warning. Beth, listen to me," said Jordan, "you have absolutely nothing to go on here. There must have been a terrible fight and someone was hurt. Yes, that was all very odd the other night when Mildred was hit – but – there is no missing person. No body, no evidence of anything. Let it go."

"What about the blood in Monty's hair? How do we explain that?" Beth seemed almost desperate to keep this investigation alive.

"How do you know it isn't blood from the fish?" Monty piped up, now feeling reassured that he hadn't been lying in the blood of a dead man.

"We don't know, Monty. We don't know anything. All that we can be sure of is that someone or some people do not want you anywhere near the Hall. I'd do just that. Stay away." Jordan wanted to make them all understand that this was really serious. Possibly not dead man serious, but serious enough that people didn't want them around.

"Beth, I will be home in about three weeks. Let the dust settle until I come home. If then, you want to talk about everything and maybe we get the police involved, then at least I'm there. Please don't do anything more when I'm the other side of the world and at least a day away from getting to you."

"OK," said Beth. "I know you're right and I'll stay out of trouble. I won't do anything you don't want me to and I won't talk to anyone about this. I love you."

"Love you too. I'm still not happy that someone has been to the house in the dark again and managed to scare you all – again. Just promise me you'll call the police if there's anything else that happens, because if there is and you haven't been meddling anywhere you shouldn't be meddling, then we *do* have a problem. At that point, I will be straight home."

The pair of chums, who had previously had so much fun trotting around old houses and derelict hovels looking for spooks and spectres, now stood looking into a bin full of fish body parts and slime.

"Well, that was a fun way to start the day." Monty was now standing significantly far enough away so as not to gag at the smell.

"Something's still not right, Monty."

"No, Beth; you promised Jordan."

"That's right, I did. I said *I* wouldn't do anything or go anywhere near, but I didn't promise *you* wouldn't."

Auntie Mildred had been listening to their conversation.

"OK, you two, I want to talk to you in the snug. Did you put the lid back on the bin, Beth?"

Beth nodded, also confirming she had locked the back door.

Auntie Mildred, Monty, Beth and a bottle of brandy (just two glasses, Beth noticed) followed each other into the snug.

Auntie Mildred stood by the fire. She had a pen in her hand and Beth suddenly realised she had stuck an A1 sheet of paper on the wall. Jordan would have gone mad had he been here – this paper was used only for his mining work.

Beth, however, suddenly felt that Auntie Mildred was going to get herself involved in their sleuthing.

Having her on side, Beth thought, outnumbered Monty so, all of sudden, she felt that familiar rush of excitement.

"I had a phone call earlier from Flora, the nurse from the other evening. What a lovely young lady. Just checking I was OK. When she was talking to me, she didn't sound particularly happy so I have asked her over for dinner tonight. I think something's not right there and I think we need to know what it is."

"What the bloody hell did you do that for, Auntie Mildred? This is just lunacy. You *do* realise, don't you…" Monty stood up, but sat down quicker than he had stood up as Menacing Mildred walked towards him.

"…You *do* realise that you are supposed to own this house, be the neighbour – this is our cover, so that we… Beth, preferably, can snoop around that dreadful house to try to unravel this mess."

Replacing her biro for a marker pen, Auntie Mildred looked at them both. Her face was unsmiling (which wasn't unusual), with one hand on her hip holding the pen and the other now holding a glass of brandy. She began.

"Monty, Beth, whilst I cannot say that I am here under duress, the exact opposite, actually. I don't think I have had more excitement in my life since I was attacked in a shop in Cape Town in 1983 – a case of mistaken identity, but terribly scary nonetheless. No, I am here because I want to see this out. Find out who attacked me and knock out the rest of his teeth. I do believe, the night you were there on your ghost hunt, you witnessed someone being killed. The reason I am confident in saying this is that no-one, or rather, people do not do the things that they are doing to us/me unless they want to scare you away. Now, we have no body, no mention of a missing person, absolutely no evidence of anything other than what you saw that night and the things that have happened since. So, the reason for asking Flora to come round this evening is to get to know a little more about her family. We will dine in the kitchen – there's nothing in there that would suggest who owns the house – and, other than the photo of John Travolta in the loo, I think it's OK for her to come round. There was, was there not, a large event at the Hall on that night, so probably everyone other than the two men you heard talking would be chatting and too interested in social climbing to notice if anyone went missing for a little while.

I am very keen to learn more and I think she is a good place to start. Beth, you are going to drive Monty and myself to the pub early afternoon. We will be seen out and about, but I want you both to have your eyes peeled. See if anyone's taking any notice of us – other than Bert and his bulbous belly. Monty, you need to relax a little because every time anyone looks at you, you look like you want to cry out for your mother. Grab hold of what your daddy gave you and let's get to the bottom of this motherfucking situation."

Both Beth and Monty burst out laughing.

"Auntie Mildred!" exclaimed Monty.

Even Auntie Mildred was laughing. "I got that line from a Samuel L Jackson film. *Snakes on a Plane*, I think." Auntie Mildred, the film buff, always had a line from a film tucked up her sleeve. This particular one was when you knew the snakes were behind the door to the cockpit and were just waiting to pounce as soon as the door was opened.

It was all about the anticipation.

"What's the paper on the wall for, Auntie Mildred?" asked Beth.

Auntie Mildred began to draw. Beth noticed that she seemed to have a rather artistic hand.

Drawing a large house and a second house, which was, Beth guessed, the Gate House, she then walked to Beth and handed her the marker pen.

"Now, Beth, thinking about where you went on that first night, try to map out the route of the tunnels."

With her less than artistic hand, Beth mapped out the yard and the stabling area where they began their journey. She was picturing, in her mind's eye, the tunnel they went through, bringing them underneath the 'Incident Room'.

Beth then began the route, which led them to the surface.

Following this, she drew the tunnel from the Gate House to the area where she found the bin.

Standing back from the wall, they all looked at the maze of lines.

"I believe there is a massive network of tunnels we haven't tapped into and my guess is the body could be lying anywhere in there or buried," Beth determined.

In truth, this wasn't great guesswork by Beth as it was actually Lady Flora who had made the statement in a passing comment.

"Isn't this really a job for the police or am I missing something here? When did we become Agatha Christie and co? I, for one, value my life and, given that I'm planning to be around for many years to come, I'm just not seeing what we can do and even less picturing this ending well. Just saying." Monty sensed they would be heading back there at some point and he wasn't sure just how much 'manpower' he had left in him.

"Monty, let's just imagine – again – that no-one actually died that night. If we bring in the police then we have absolutely nothing to go on other than us actually snooping around someone else's property. Until we have something tangible to show them, we have to continue snooping and questioning. Oh, and before you say anything about Jordan and my promise – don't bother!"

Beth felt this was the time that she had dreamed of from a very early age. Most of her father's friends and relatives of her own close friends had farms. A farm, to Beth, spelled adventure.

From the cockerel who used to chase Beth and her friend Herb (pet name given to Dianne by her family) around the farm. No-one believed that they feared for their lives until Herb's grandfather who owned the farm actually saw this monster chasing them with devilish intentions. This went on for months, every Saturday following their guitar lessons. They would go to the farm, drop off their guitars and go to find that particular week's adventure. There it would be, black as night, eyes shining as it glared at them, in wait. Who would make the first move? One step from either Beth or Herb and the chase would begin. The final straw, which ultimately, saw the end of this devilish beast, came one Saturday following a chase that seemed to last forever. Beth noticed two very large wicker baskets by the side of the cowshed, opposite the pigsty, which used to be the resting place for this bird of prey. Beth and Herb, who had noticed the same basket, dived in and pulled over the lid. The bird sat on the lid for over an hour and they sat inside wondering if they would ever be found.

Herb's grandfather had seen it all. Once he had stopped smiling, he took the bird away. The two girls would have to find adventure elsewhere.

Beth knew, from that point on, that she must have adventure or mystery in her life. This was the reason she took up ghost hunting. Always hopeful that one day (or better still, one night) there would be a sighting and she would have to run for her life, just as she had all those years ago. She realised now that the cockerel had unwittingly ignited her arteries, filling them with adventure that flowed within her. That same adrenaline was what she was feeling today.

"I'm in, Auntie Mildred." Beth shook her hand.

Monty stood up with a little more confidence now. "Me, too," also shaking the hand of his very elderly aunt. How could he not be? He needed to prove to her, and probably himself too, that he did not need to hide behind his mother's skirt. After all, Auntie Mildred's would do just as well.

CHAPTER TEN

Beth had dressed in jeans, ankle boots and a pink jumper that she then replaced with a navy one – if their job was to see who took notice of them, she didn't want her jumper to be a potential reason (it was bright, bright pink but she loved it).

Monty, how she loved her dear friend, was a traditional dresser. Loafers, white shirt, delicate pink jumper and bright red jeans. He always looked very smart. Beth, when she first saw him, thought he was a member of the royal family. He has a lovely manner, is quietly spoken and articulate with a wit that is as sharp as any razor.

Today, true to his own self, he did not disappoint.

"Monty, don't you think those trousers may attract unwanted attention? They're a bit… Loud."

Without a word, Monty went to change. He did this only because he, too, thought they might be a little 'stand out'.

Auntie Mildred walked in, quite the opposite to Monty. She was dressed from head to toe in black. Her usual glasses were replaced with larger, black-rimmed frames. Beth actually looked at her, thinking, *I hope I dress like you when I'm that old.* Her shoes, however, seemed to let her down. They were so old-fashioned.

Auntie Mildred seemed to read her mind.

"The shoes are practical, my darling. I only wear these when I'm expected to be on my feet for longer periods. Where's Monty?"

"Oh, he went to change his trousers, hopefully into something that isn't quite so fluorescent."

Monty realised he needed to consider his colourful wardrobe during events such as he found himself in right now. How the hell do you blend in when you have several pairs of trousers – all the same bar the colour, but equally as bright? He eventually decided on a pair of jeans. He didn't really like ordinary denim jeans; he felt drab and samey. Still, today, drab and samey seemed to be in order.

As he walked into the kitchen, he received approving looks from both ladies.

Driving to the pub, Beth realised that the events of the day so far, suddenly seemed acceptable. No-one really spoke during the relatively short drive. Auntie Mildred had a bit of a coughing fit, so Monty slapped her back and she slapped his hand.

"My bones are not bars of steel, you bloody fool!"

"You can choke to death next time." Monty was, as always, stunned by the sucker punch remarks dealt by his aunt. She just never seemed to appreciate help of any kind, apart from Beth helping her with her top the other night. Of course, he hadn't said those words out loud. He didn't dare.

Predictably, inside the busy pub, Burt was the first to greet them. Jumping awkwardly from the bar stool, he came over, kissed Auntie Mildred's hand and guided her to a table in the middle of the restaurant rather than what had become their usual corner table.

"Drinks, everyone?" Burt's ruddier than usual complexion, Beth thought, was due to their early afternoon seating; he had obviously been on it for the last few hours.

"If there's anything left, yes we will," Auntie Mildred had replied. *There she goes again*, thought Monty.

A young girl came to take their drinks order, but a different one from before. Auntie Mildred asked for a menu and then commented that there should have been one on the table already. Once again, another young girl walked away bruised by her words. Bio-Oil couldn't help *her*. Beth observed the young girl who'd had the spat with Auntie Mildred the last time they were in. She was on duty, but had quite wisely decided to tend to another table.

"Anyone in of interest?" asked Auntie Mildred whilst scouring the room and smiling as she did.

"Haven't seen anyone so far," replied Monty, "but we have only just come in."

Following their first drink and having placed an order for the next round and, thankfully, some lunch too, Monty announced he needed the loo.

As he walked across the room, Beth found herself looking to see if anyone was looking at him. No-one was. With that, she resumed her conversation with Auntie Mildred about Beth's plans to extend the unused chicken coop in her garden in readiness for the purchase of the point of lays Jordan was yet to be made aware of.

Monty found it inconceivable that any man could stand against a wall and pee into a ceramic bowl. He thought that was utterly disgusting. He always used a cubicle.

Just prior to flushing, he heard the door go. This, in his opinion, was not noteworthy, but that was until he heard two men talking.

"Have you seen who's in here with a young woman?"

"Yes, the old bitch."

Monty sat on the toilet lid and, quite frankly, had no idea how he was to deal with this situation. Where the hell was his mother's skirt when he needed it?

"I think we need to sort her out once and for all. If she hasn't been scared off so far, then we'll have to speak with the boss and see what he wants us to do."

With that, they both walked out.

The oddest thing was that Monty's first thought was that they hadn't washed their hands. Reality now kicking in, he decided once he'd washed his, he would see who was weaving through the seating inside the restaurant, only to find he had left it too late. He also found himself thinking how brazen they were, not checking to see if anyone else was in the bathroom.

The men, he thought, were not riff-raff, but nor were they gentry. Another thought very quickly came to his mind, which was that they didn't mention the old bitch being with a young woman and a young man. It was at this point his detective skills came in handy. He decided to walk out of the pub and begin to walk back to Beth's house. No-one suspected him so he thought it best to keep it that way. If no-one suspected him, why put himself up there to be shot at?

Calling Beth, who had assumed Monty was ill and had asked one of the barmen to go in to the loo to see if he was OK, she found herself picking up the phone, not really understanding what was going on. Why was he calling her and where was he?

Monty explained what had happened. His suggestion was that they continue with their lunch and say nothing to Auntie Mildred until they were in the car. They could pick Monty up on the way back if he wasn't already home. Monty felt he needed to think.

Beth felt that they needed to leave. Quickly.

Auntie Mildred had, however, ordered the largest burger Beth had ever seen. That said, she seemed to be making short work of getting through it.

Beth was eating salad. Picking at it, at best. She had no appetite.

"Where's Monty?" Auntie Mildred asked.

"He's outside. I don't think he's feeling very well. We should probably go and get him home."

Feeling slightly disappointed, Auntie Mildred decided that she was probably right. The focus for the rest of the day had to be Flora and what information they could get out of her that evening.

Burt, for all of his best efforts, could not persuade Auntie Mildred to stay. He thought she was 'a sort' and was sure she could show him a good time.

Auntie Mildred, slightly flattered by his attention, could think of nothing worse than jumping into bed with him. At her age, however, she was still probably 100 times more agile than him. Now, if he lost a few stone, she probably would!

Leaving the pub, Auntie Mildred scoured the car park. She couldn't see Monty anywhere.

In the car, Beth explained what had happened. Auntie Mildred, Beth thought, seemed to be a little taken aback by this news.

"What the hell does that mean? Deal with me 'once and for all'? Let's get home, Beth, and discuss this over the third drink we didn't have in the pub."

They found Monty walking alongside a field. He was picking wild flowers, which he had arranged in his hand in a rather artistic way. He'd always liked to arrange flowers. That had been his one job at home as a young boy. Whenever Auntie Mildred or any of the other sisters would come for afternoon tea, he would be responsible for going into the garden and creating a lovely centrepiece for the table.

He knew which flowers never to pick. His mother had flowers that were her prized possessions. He'd fallen foul of that once. It never happened again.

As Monty got into the car, Auntie Mildred actually praised him for his forward thinking.

"Good work in there, Monty, my boy."

Now that was a first!

Back home, they sat around the kitchen table. Auntie Mildred brought in the rest of the brandy. This time, only one glass, which was obviously meant for her. She could think well with a brandy at hand.

Monty had white wine, feeling as though he had missed out in the pub and Beth had tonic water; she actually hated to drink during the day.

Moving towards the toaster, Beth put a couple of slices in for Monty who loved hot, buttered toast and, after all, he'd missed out on a meal.

Monty relayed the entire conversation he had overheard whilst eating his toast.

"Are you both sure you can't recall who came out of the gents before me?"

Neither of them could.

"Look, Auntie Mildred, you will never be in a situation where you are alone at any point, so whatever is planned for you, they'll have to get through us first." Beth seemed quite defiant.

This was hardly the defence barrier Auntie Mildred was comfortable with, but it would have to do.

"Then let them come to us!" announced Auntie Mildred.

"This isn't bloody Zulu, Auntie Mildred. If, and I know at this stage it's only an if, if someone *was* killed, this is very serious stuff. We need to really think about this. What is our actual plan, Agatha and Nancy Drew?"

Now it was Beth's turn to stand up.

"OK, here's our plan. Flora is coming round tonight. Let me lead the questions, please. Once she has gone home, let's see if we have gained any info or whether we just had a pleasant evening with a lovely girl who has a shit home life."

That seemed like a fair plan, they all decided.

Changing into their casuals or their combat gear Beth felt best described their evening look, Auntie Mildred rustled up a dish that smelled divine. Rice, peas, prawns (where the hell did she find them?) and a whole host of herbs and spices. *Wow*, thought Beth, *she can really cook*.

Flora had decided to walk to Mildred's house, not really thinking about how she would get home. Hopefully, she would get really pissed and just wake up tomorrow in her own bed. Two days off, but, for her, that was not something she cherished. Growing up, she had never been encouraged to bring friends home. Had she been, she probably wouldn't have invited anyone anyway. Her parents were a constant embarrassment to her. They were rude to each other and they were dismissive of their children. Not so much her mother but her father, for sure.

Flora had hated her father for years. Looking back, she thought she had actually disliked him from the very beginning. As she began to grow up and understand her family heritage, she learned very quickly that her mother's privilege was her father's entitlement – at least that was his understanding of what he had married into.

Her mother's family purse amounted to hundreds of millions of pounds. This was protected by a family trust. Flora's father received a monthly allowance. They all did. Flora put hers into an account, her brother put his up his nose and their father, well, who knew how he spent his, but this, to her father, was an insult. "That can't be love," he would tell his wife. For years he had tried to quash the trust. His wife would not hear of it. Deep down, she decided that her husband didn't love her; he had probably never loved her. What he had loved was her money, a fact he rarely denied these days.

Flora's brother, Felix, was a victim of his family's behaviour. Flora had decided to throw herself into work while Felix threw himself into the London party life. His money made him popular and he mistook this for friendship.

Flora disliked her brother almost as much as she did her father.

Growing up, her time at home was fairly limited given that she had been a boarder at school. When she was at home, she had tried to avoid her father as much as she could. He had always seemed irritated by her and she couldn't understand why. She loved to read, always wanted to learn and she was caring – which of these things could a father *not* love about his daughter?

Flora had once overheard her father talking to someone on the phone. It had been a woman and Flora knew for sure that they had some kind of relationship between them, but decided there was little point raising this with him and she certainly wouldn't upset her mother who, being equally astute, would surely know this already.

There was no affection towards Flora from Lord Grey; he was incapable of caring about anyone or anything. She hated the way he spoke to their staff. He was cutting and these people had worked there for years. He appreciated no-one.

Unfortunately, these traits were passed down to her brother. Master Felix had no time for his sister. She didn't smoke, hardly drank and she actually had a job. Even as a young girl, Flora would help out in the garden, earning her weekly pocket money. Felix just took his.

Years of this behaviour from as far back as she could remember, killed any feelings she had for either her father or her brother.

Her mother was a lovely woman and Flora could only imagine the awful years she experienced growing up. Her grandmother and grandfather were obsessed with society and their place in it. Lady Grey was their only child and, boy, did they ring fence her heritage. Flora suspected they had the measure of her father. That was their best move ever and her father hated them for their ace move.

Now they were gone.

Flora's mother merely existed, a prisoner almost. Trapped

because of her heritage. This saddened Flora. Her mother found comfort in her longstanding friendship with Agnes and also her love for her garden.

Flora's lack of interaction with people her own age meant she had few meaningful relationships in her own life. Valuing her friendship with Agnes, she had hoped some of her confidences were fed back to her mother that, in Flora's mind, may in the future, strengthen the bond between mother and daughter.

Flora also found herself growing fond of Frank. They had a gentle friendship, which she valued. He had no idea about how she felt and she was certainly not ready to expose her feelings towards him. Agnes was aware, but Flora was too scared to admit it to Frank in case it ruined their friendship and he didn't feel the same – that could ruin everything for him. She felt Frank was strong and worldly-wise; these were not characteristics Flora recognised in herself.

Flora welcomed the arrival of Auntie Mildred and her relatives because Beth seemed really easy to talk to. She was very funny and seemed to have a lifetime of stories Flora found both interesting and hilarious. They could be great friends but, as always, these good people rarely stayed long in Flora's life.

As she reached the house, Flora could smell, almost immediately, the most awful stench of rotting fish.

What the hell!

As she knocked on the front door, she saw Beth coming round the corner of the house.

"Auntie Mildred says friends always come in through the kitchen." This was actually Beth's own rule of thumb.

The two walked into the kitchen.

"What a lovely, yummy smell, Mildred," said Flora.

They all sat down to eat; Flora had brought bottles of both red and white wine.

"I love your flowers, Mildred," Flora commented on the arrangement on the table.

"Monty picked them earlier on his way back from the pub."

"They're lovely. Monty. You have an eye for arranging."

Monty blushed and thanked her. Secretly, he found Flora to be delightful.

They ate and drank and drank some more.

"So, Flora, what do you do to unwind on your days off?" Beth was straight in.

"I generally don't unwind. In truth, I tend to work, then sleep and, on my day off, I usually put myself up for extra shifts."

Quizzing her on this, it became obvious that Flora held no love for her heritage. Loving her family home, Waterdale Hall, which was a magnificent property, Flora felt that since it was such an old building, the public should be able to visit and learn more about its history.

"Do people around here know about the tunnel network beneath the Hall?"

"No, this isn't something that has ever been exposed. I, for one, wouldn't want that."

Well, someone knows, thought Beth.

Delving deeper…

"Didn't you venture down there when you were a kid?"

"Never. Who would I go on such an adventure with? My friends never came here."

"Not even with your brother?"

"No, not even with him. We didn't have that kind of relationship."

"Such an adventure for a child. Do you ever feel that you missed out on your childhood?"

Beth was asking her a genuine question. This wasn't part of her interrogation.

"Beth, I have missed out on so much more."

Auntie Mildred was in tears, for Flora and for herself. Her own childhood was as crap as Flora had described her own as being.

Auntie Mildred found that she was suddenly analysing herself. Why was she so brusque? So unfeeling towards almost everyone, almost everyone but never Monty. Why was that? As if this was the unveiling of a new painting at a gallery, Auntie Mildred realised that it was because she had wanted Monty to have someone. She knew it would not be his mother. Monty's mother, her sister, was lost in her heritage. She had succumbed to that life. Auntie Mildred had always been fond of Monty; it was for her to be there for him. He was, to some, a social butterfly, he would write his columns in the most informed, articulate way, but then there was this Monty, out of his comfort zone, needing the protection he'd never had. Auntie Mildred was sure that she would die to protect her nephew, her beloved Monty. Well, maybe not jump in front of a train or even a double-decker, but definitely a pushbike or a six-foot menace. She knew how to use her cosh now.

As Flora stood up to go home, Beth had offered to drive her. How could she not? Flora had, after all, gone out of her way to check Auntie Mildred was OK.

No way was she going to let her walk home. Although Beth knew she had been drinking, it was such a short drive along an actual road, she would take a chance to protect her friend.

In the car, Flora was adamant that she could walk home. Beth had pressed the mute button a while ago.

"Are you staying in the Gate House with Agnes?"

"No, the main house. Mum's home alone so I'll stay with her. She'll be asleep, but at least I know I'll be there for her."

Beth smiled.

Flora waved her goodbye and Beth reversed to go back up the driveway. There it was, the figure – tall and looming. It wasn't for herself that she feared, it was Flora.

"Flora!" she shouted, with her head out the window.

Flora walked back to the car.

"Shall I walk you to the door?"

"Why?"

"I thought I saw someone standing beside the house."

Flora laughed. "That'll be one of the security guys." She laughed again. "Don't worry, I've lived here forever."

Beth watched her friend talk to the guy, then walk into the house. The last week or so had made her paranoid.

Driving home, albeit a hundred yards, she found herself thinking about Flora's life. How different was her own life. Filled with love, laughter and friendship. Beth had loved her entire life and loved it still.

Pulling into her drive, she parked her car. Locked the door. Heard the electric gates close. Walked into the house. Locked the kitchen door.

And then…

The security light came on in the garden.

Standing right beside the tree was the tallest figure she had ever seen. He was wearing what looked like a onesie. A very big onesie to cover his very big body.

He was looking straight at her.

She looked right back at him. Who would move first?

Someone turned off the kitchen light.

"Beth, someone's in the garden."

"For fuck's sake, Monty, I know. I was staring straight at him and then you turned off the light."

"Er, no, I didn't. I haven't touched anything."

"Oh. Then who did?"

They ran into the sitting room where Auntie Mildred was sat watching the garden; it obviously wasn't her. Beth realised in an instant that someone had cut the power. The light surrounding the fireplace was also off. This light was never off. Looking at Auntie Mildred, Beth realised that she was asleep.

"Monty, check all the doors and windows downstairs. I'll do the same upstairs."

"Beth, I think I'm a little bit scared right now." Monty didn't mind admitting this.

"Monty, so am I." Beth was unashamed to admit the same.

Establishing all windows and doors were locked, they took Auntie Mildred up to her room.

"Monty, don't be alarmed by what I am about to say, but I think we all need to sleep in the same room tonight. We can barricade ourselves in and both you and I can keep watch."

Monty was not alarmed; in fact, he was warmed by this suggestion.

Auntie Mildred, face planted in her bed, was snoring louder than any beast domestic or wild.

Monty took the opportunity to sleep first. He lay on the chaise longue and, within minutes, he too found his slumber.

Beth sat in a chair for a moment. Then she stood by the window looking into the garden. What was she expecting to find in there? Whatever it was, she couldn't see it.

Two hours later, it was Monty's turn to keep watch.

Beth prodded him. He was completely unhappy to be awoken.

"Come on, Monty, I have been awake the last two hours, it's your turn now."

"What if I see someone?"

"Then wake me up, you idiot. Goodnight."

Within moments, Beth was asleep. Monty decided to read a book about sharks.

It was Auntie Mildred who woke up next.

"What the hell?" she exclaimed as she looked to her left then her right.

Beth lay to her left, Monty to her right. Both were asleep.

Smiling to herself, she dozed off, as any loving mother would do.

An abrupt banging on the bedroom door woke all three. Beth grabbed the book on sharks (why was this out?) and Monty flung the door open so that Beth could whack the intruder.

With a firm blow to the head, Beth had felt surprisingly victorious.

"Beth, what the hell?"

Jordan stood in the doorway nursing what would definitely become a large bruise over the next hour or so.

Holy shit. It was Jordan. How could they explain spending the night in Auntie Mildred's room without the confession of what they, no – she – had been up to? After all, it was only her who had to explain herself to him.

"Hey, you."

Jordan, who knew this was trouble, smiled at his wife. He loved her. She was safe, so were the others; he would question later, but for now, he would just love her and be happy that she was safe."

"Hey, you too. What' been going on?"

"Fancy a coffee? I know I do," said Beth. Monty was so relieved to see Jordan. The only person in this house who had any sense!

"I'll get the coffee going," offered Monty.

They left Auntie Mildred to sleep. Realising the cavalry had returned, she turned over with the feeling that she could be excused for the next couple of hours (at least).

"So, I'm guessing there's a really good explanation for the three of you sleeping in the same room… I don't know, something like the boiler packed up and you were all cold or maybe Mildred had a bad dream? What I'm hoping it's not, is that you decided to carry on with your snooping around and something scared you into one room? What's it to be?"

"So, over to you Beth!" Monty was relieved he didn't have to explain this one away.

Making a coffee for everyone, listening to Beth's recollection of events and watching Jordan's face, Monty didn't speak.

Probably for the first time during this sequence of events, he now felt it was their duty to solve this mystery. His friend was right, – they couldn't go to the police, at least not until they had something solid to go on.

Even more surprising was Jordan's response to all of this.

"OK, then, let's be rid of the fish guts. Even with the lid on that bin, it stinks out there. Then, I think we need to go back down that tunnel, possibly both tunnels, and see if we can find anything at all that gets us somewhere."

Beth was overjoyed. This was what she was hoping for. A united front.

"What shall we do with the fish guts?" Monty was relieved they would be going; the stench made him wretch.

"I haven't got that far yet, Monty. Perhaps you and I can move it to the bottom of the garden for now. No-one goes down there and the neighbours are too far away for it to be a problem for them."

That will do, Monty thought.

After their coffee, Jordan, who seemed to get a second wind following his fabulous sleep on the plane, went outside to see just how heavy the bin actually was.

It was as heavy as he'd been told. They decided that the only way of moving it sensibly would be to lift the bin and empty the contents into a wheelbarrow. Beth, although she was a toughie, was no match for such a weight and Monty, well, it was fair to say that a single glance at him told you he wouldn't be of any use.

It was decided, much to Monty's absolute disgust, that they would try to lift it between the three of them.

Actually, it was Monty who came up with the marvellous idea of creating shallow steps out of old bricks and to lift it that way. This worked a treat. Now they just had to manoeuvre it down the garden, which was not as level as any of them had hoped it would be.

Reaching the bottom of the garden, it became obvious to all that the bricks were no longer handy and each acknowledged that bringing them down the garden to do the same job in reverse was going to be too much trouble.

They looked at each other.

"We can do this!" Beth announced.

"I hope you're only talking to Jordan when you say that, Beth." Monty was repulsed once again.

"Don't be a drip, Monty. It's just a 'one, two, three – lift' situation and down it goes."

Monty stuck two fingers up at Beth and turned to Jordan.

"Please can you direct this, Jordan. I have no faith in Beth at all and even less in myself."

They each stood, legs slightly apart and bent a little.

On the nod, they were instructed to lift with their fingers under the rim of the actual bin and not the lid.

They had been given the nod. Up it went; moving away from the wheelbarrow, they inched across the lawn. Until they decided how to dispose of the contents, the resting place was to be in the corner.

Then, the worst thing that could have happened, actually happened. Monty twisted his ankle on a large stone. Trying to stay balanced, he yanked the bin towards him, which put both Beth and Jordan out of sync and over they all went.

Monty was the first to hit the floor, next was the bin, then the lid and then the contents of the bin. He was submerged in dead fish.

Beth and Jordan managed to escape any splashback.

Beth thought she heard Monty cry.

His hands were covering his mouth, slime and crap was dripping down his face and he had a fish head on top of his own.

Jordan looked at Beth.

"Go to the house, get some towels and a bucket of water."

Beth continued to stare at Monty; she didn't know whether to laugh, which would have been her first instinct, or cry. She knew Monty would be so upset if only he could speak.

Running as fast as she could up her long garden and into the airing cupboard, she searched for the oldest towels she could find.

Back outside, she filled the bucket with water and, as gracefully as she could, she walked back down the garden to where the boys remained – neither seemed to have moved.

Jordan dipped one of the towels into the water and wiped Monty's face. Beth did the same for his head.

Jordan told Monty to cover his nose and mouth and proceeded to throw the bucket of water over his head. You could now see his face. Beth wiped his hair with a dry towel.

"Beth," began Monty, "when I can eventually open my eyes, I never want to see you again."

"Let's get you to the hosepipe, Monty, and wash this shit off you."

"The hosepipe? Are you joking?"

Jordan was absolutely not joking. Whilst he was sympathetic to Monty's state, there was no way he would be going into the house until he was, a) fish free, and b) undressed.

"I've seen this in films!" Monty shouted. "Films about victims of terror – *Waterboarding Jordan* – that's what this is."

Beth handed him an old dressing gown.

"I ran you a bath, Monty. It smells lovely. Go and get in it, get dressed and I'll rustle up something to eat."

Monty said nothing. He looked at her and for the first time he could see she was genuinely upset for him.

"What shall you do with my clothes? Oh, and Beth, I'll eat anything, but no fish!"

"I'll hose them down, then wash them and no fish, Monty. I wouldn't dare." Beth had an old washing machine in the garage that she used for her walking coats and trainers. She'd be using that. First, meanwhile, she had to wash off his clothes. She found herself gagging.

Off went Monty to his sea of bubbles.

Jordan looked at his wife.

"Yet another surprisingly quiet day I've returned home to."

They smiled at each other.

"I'll help you with his clothes."

"Shall we have a cup of tea first? I kind of need one. Is it just me or was that one of the funniest things you've ever seen in your life? Priceless, Beth, but you can't ever tell him that. I think I heard him cry."

Poor Monty.

CHAPTER ELEVEN

Monty loved a bath.

He had decided to shower first, get rid of what the hose hadn't and then he would get into his sea of scent. He had to admit; it did smell fabulous.

As he lay there, he started to think about his new wardrobe – his lovely jumpers; one full of holes from his hedge experience, another full of fish that would probably only fit a small child once Beth had washed it. He decided he would put a claim in to Beth once this business was done with.

Jordan and Beth were in the garden hosing down the clothes, his shoes, socks, pants; bloody hell, this stuff was everywhere, but then there had been an 'offal' lot of it.

"I think, Beth, if you hold up the jumper and trousers, I can do a better job with the hose."

Just before they put everything in the washing machine (ignoring any care labels), Beth did her usual trick of checking the pockets. This was an exercise she always did, nowadays at least. She had washed Jordan's jeans a couple of years ago without realising he had about £100 in one of the pockets. A costly mistake she would not repeat. She did manage to dry the cash out, but wasn't prepared to take any chances from that point onwards.

Putting her hand in the front pocket, she screamed out.

"Ah, ugh, Jordan, there's a fish head in the pocket!" She threw the trousers down onto the floor and ran around like a child.

Jordan picked up the trousers.

"Beth, really!"

Putting his hand into the pocket, he lifted out the fish, only to find it wasn't a fish. It was a finger. A human finger.

At that moment, Monty walked out of the kitchen door. He felt very clean and smelled very fresh.

"Oh, that's so much better." Given the events over the past hour-and-a-half hours, he felt remarkably cheerful.

"What's up, and where's Auntie Mildred?" The instant he saw the faces of his two friends, he was less cheery. He sensed something bad had just happened.

"What the hell is that?" Monty was looking at the finger that was now lying on the grass. He clearly knew what it was.

They all looked at each other.

"OK," began Jordan, "if they had wanted to scare you with a bin load of guts, why would they put a finger in there that could easily have been missed? We need to go through what's down in the garden to see if there's anything else. This is what we need to go to the police with. Beth, go and tell Auntie Mildred we have found something. Don't tell her what it is yet, but tell her to stay indoors and lock all of the doors following last night's incident."

Jordan had been into the kitchen, returning with a freezer bag for the finger, which he then picked up with a pair of oven gloves.

Monty put the oven gloves in the wheelie bin.

Jordan handed Monty a face mask – he had lots of these that he used when he went into his mines. Not brilliant, but quite effective. Monty sprayed his with his mouth freshener.

Walking down the garden, he could hardly believe that not 20 minutes ago, he was swilling around in aquatic luxury and now he was heading back to the very shit he'd just washed off.

They each had a garden fork, which they were turning over to rake through the fish parts to check for any human remains. After what seemed like an age, Jordan looked to Monty.

"Where's Beth?"

"Probably having tea and toast with Auntie. You know Beth."

"Yes, I do, but I know that she would not want to miss out on something being found and her not being involved."

Right on cue, Beth was racing down the garden. Initially, they couldn't make out what she was saying, but eventually she was close enough.

"I can't find her!"

Auntie Mildred was not in the house.

Each of them were shouting her name and checking all the rooms once again.

Nothing.

Beth checked her bedroom and bathroom.

She'd obviously got dressed, but hadn't showered, nor had she brushed her teeth. Since these were the two very things she did every morning without fail, Beth became very anxious for the well-being of this little old lady.

Walking into the kitchen, Beth told the others of the situation.

"Do we report her as a missing person?" Monty's voice was almost a whimper.

"Not yet," replied Jordan. "It's too soon. How do we know she didn't go for a walk?"

They walked into her room.

Her clothes were folded; her bed was made. The vase with one rose in it still stood upright beside her bed.

Whatever happened had happened in a very civilised manner.

"We are going down those tunnels tonight."

"She won't be down a tunnel, Jordan, she's in her 80s. "

"I'm not expecting her to be, Monty. I think there's more to this underworld than you have seen so far."

It was early afternoon. The sky was as black as night, but it wasn't night. Not yet. They would have to wait.

Jordan had found his navy blue jumpsuit he used to fix the car with. He gave this to Monty. Beth had something similar she used for gardening in winter. This left Jordan with his Lycra skin-tight running bottoms – hardly ideal, but would allow him to move easily. All of them had trainers – Jordan had to give Monty a pair when he realised his were bright orange. They didn't really fit Monty, they were slightly too big, but he didn't say so. They all wore balaclavas (these were Jordan's, which, again, he wore when mining and they were Lycra. The helmets miners had to wear came off much easier with the balaclava underneath).

Now they needed their plan.

This is where Beth took control.

"The tunnels, we know, can be accessed from the three points we know of, so we will have to take one each – beside the Gate House, by the woods and then the one in the stables that we went down on that first night, Monty. I'll go that way because Jordan doesn't know about that one and there's probably more chance of someone being around that area. No offence, Monty, but I think I will think on my feet much quicker than you."

Monty certainly took no offence. He had no intentions of going back that way. In truth, he didn't want to go *any* way, but his aunt – lovely, but scary Auntie Mildred – had been taken and he owed it to her to help find her.

Nightfall came around very slowly.

Beth had tied her hair into a knot on top of her head. She had worn a balaclava before and had that experience to call upon. Sweating like a bitch, she knew how to keep cool this time around. Putting on her all-in-one, she had decided to wear her gym kit underneath for the same reasons. There was nothing worse than needing to stay cool when you were sweating.

Jordan, well, he was just cool anyway. He just looked like he was going to the gym with a long-sleeved top on. He knew how to stay cool. He even wore his balaclava in a way that made him look even cooler.

Monty had no past experiences to call upon. Deciding that a night-time event would be a cold affair, the temperature dropped after dark – everyone knew this. He decided to wear his long johns. He didn't bring them intentionally. It was more of a habit. For some reason, he always seemed to need them. Today was such an occasion. Should he wear his last remaining jumper? Daffodil yellow and injury-free. He decided against this; instead, he chose a shirt, which he knew may prove to be a little too much but he thought perhaps if the temperature dropped enough, it would prove to be a winning choice. Obviously, he had Jordan's trainers. A little too big, but with his thermal socks (actually they were Auntie Mildred's) he reckoned if he wore them, he stood a better chance of finding her. Pulling on the all-in-one, he'd wished he had put the trainers on last… it was proving troublesome pulling the outfit over the trainers. Eventually on, he had to give himself a minute to recover. Bloody hell, he was extremely hot!

"Where's Monty?" *Jordan looks so flippin' hot*, thought Beth as she walked into the kitchen.

"If anyone stands a chance of solving this, it's you, Beth," commented Jordan, looking at his wife. She looked like a ninja. "No idea, by the way. He went to get changed."

"Monty! Let's run through the plan again. It's almost time to go."

Run through the plan again? thought Monty. *Did we run through it already?* He thought they'd just discussed access points to the tunnels.

Flustered and hot once more, Monty walked into the Kitchen. The Aga was not his friend tonight.

He walked in and kept walking until he was standing outside.

"How do you stand that heat? It's so hot in there. Can we do this outside? I'm too hot."

"What do you have on under there, Monty?" Beth couldn't understand why he was so hot. It was hardly the middle of summer.

"None of your business, but I think I'm old enough to dress myself."

"OK. Then stop moaning."

Outside, they sat on the patio wall.

"Monty, you take the door beside the Gate House. Jordan, you take the door near the woods and I'll go in via the stable yard."

They all had their torches, the non-reflective ones.

"How can we get in touch with each other?" This was Monty's biggest concern.

"OK, here you go." Jordan handed Monty what looked like a watch.

"You can talk into it and the text comes out the other end."

"Let's try it now."

Beth picked hers up and put in on her wrist. Monty and Jordan did the same.

Dickhead, and instantly the text appeared on both Jordan's and Monty's watches.

"So childish," said Monty. Jordan just smiled.

"We can't all leave at the same time."

"I'll go first," offered Beth. "I have the farthest to go."

With that, she kissed Jordan, pinched Monty's nose and off she went.

Monty looked at Jordan.

"I know Beth has this running through her veins, but I am scared to death, Jordan. Beatings, scary conversations in toilets, fingers in my pockets, missing relatives; you know, it's just so–"

"OK, Monty, I know. Just go down the tunnel and report anything you see. If you don't see anything, come back up and hopefully one of us will have found something that connects these events."

Monty smiled at his friend.

Jordan was the next to leave the house. Locking the kitchen door before he left, Monty was about to ask how he would get back in (certain he would be the first one back), but he thought better of it.

He looked at his real watch; it was 15 minutes since Beth had left and 10 for Jordan.

It was time. He needed to leave.

Beth weaved her way through the trees until she saw the familiar pathway to the house. As she approached the house, she could hear Flora who sounded very distressed.

"I will *not* give up my job. I love it; I'm good at it. Why would I *do* that?"

"You don't need to work, for one; and for two, you could do some work around the house to help out. Your mother needs some help. This house cannot run itself."

"And you can't help out, Dad, no? Why is that? It seems to me that you'll do whatever it takes not to spend any money. And why would you? What is my brother doing with his time?"

"I don't need to do anything. That's what kids are for. We don't need any more staff draining the pot. Don't concern yourself with your brother's workload. This conversation is about you."

"Well, here's where it ends, Dad. I am a young woman who actually wants to work to help people. I will not be giving my job up, now or any time soon. I will help Mum out and I'll sort that out with her. I do not take orders from you. You are a sponge, a drain on my mother; you are zapping the life out of her. You are a lazy pig and I hate you. Go fuck yourself!"

Beth stood beside the window where this conversation was taking place.

Flora received one swift slap across her face from her father.

She didn't flinch.

"Goodbye, Dad," and with that, Flora left the room.

Beth stood in the shadows of the shrubbery so as not to be seen as Flora walked out of the house and literally right in front of her.

Phew.

What an absolute arse her dad is, thought Beth.

It didn't end there.

Lady Grey walked in after hearing the shouting between father and daughter.

"Really, you shouldn't talk to her like that! I am very proud of her. She doesn't need to work, but she chooses to. That's so refreshing."

"How ironic. *You've* never worked a day in your life! You're going to need all the help you can get when Felix and I are in London."

"London? Why are you going there?"

"I intend to shag my way around Knightsbridge, nothing younger than 30. My research has determined it could be a while until I get back."

"Please, off you go. What took you so long? And why does Felix need to go?"

"Firstly, my dull wife, it *hasn't* taken so long. I've already made a start. Felix and I are big hits in the clubs – he knows everyone. I'm sure it won't take me too long before I can stand on my own two feet. I'll be staying in the apartment."

"I hate you."

"I've hated you since the day we were married, but what can I say? You're loaded. You can't get rid of me so I've decided I'll keep taking and continue to give nothing back. Isn't that how our marriage has existed since it began? We're leaving tomorrow evening."

Lord Grey walked out of the room. Beth watched Lady Grey cry into her cardigan.

Just as she was about to slope into the barn, Beth looked up towards one of the windows in the Hall. No idea what made her do this, but what she saw sent a chill right down her spine.

The room was lit and, hanging from the curtain rail, was Auntie Mildred's cosh, presumably the one she had lost.

All of a sudden she felt very vulnerable. This was unexpected because they'd all assumed Auntie Mildred was in their sights – the fact that they'd hung this in the window suggested they knew someone was going to see it.

Sliding along the wall and into the barn, she wanted to send a message to the boys, but was fearful she would be overheard. Instead, she said nothing. Seeing the door in the corner of the room, the memory of that evening came back to her very quickly and vividly. Beth had done a great job erasing the sight of the man's face.

This was her destiny now, knowing that she had spent all these years chasing ghouls and spectres when, all along, her rightful path was solving mysteries such as this one. The other thing she knew was that this was a path she had to follow with her friend Monty. Together they were the most unlikely pairing, but they had individual strengths that seemed to bring the best from each other.

That said, she doubted very much that Monty would feel the same way after this initial sleuthing experience.

Strange that she was thinking this as she approached the doorway to the tunnel – it was as though she was giving herself a pep talk. It seemed to work.

Off she went.

Jordan felt he had the easiest of the three routes. His was the only route that wasn't positioned next to a property and he had the veil of the trees to fade into if he needed to.

Lifting the lid, he began his descent. Unfortunately for him, he didn't have the experience of 'that evening' to draw on. He felt the others at least had some expectations. He had none. Tunnels were like home to him; he'd experienced so many. Nothing like this though. This was the unknown and that, even for him, sent the nerves spinning around his stomach.

How brave was his wife!

Poor Monty! If he was brave, he kept it very well hidden.

Monty found the crawl through the hedge one of the most uncomfortable experiences of his life. He had tucked his socks into his trousers, which he had initially thought to be a great idea to avoid the bugs getting underneath. Unfortunately, the boiler suit generously donated by Jordan kept riding up his legs and his feet were getting stuck in the bulky material.

Once through and taking his trousers back out of his socks, he made his way very cautiously through the woods, heading towards the Gate House and the Gateway to Hell.

What was it about him that Beth felt was an asset to her team of two? He wasn't brave; he didn't really like the dark or the light for that matter when he felt under threat. He was, however, reliable. She knew he would always be there. And there it was, and here he is.

As he exited the trees, laying himself bare to whatever was out there, he stood still for a moment to compose his breathing. During his days in the cubs, they taught you how to stay calm in times of worry. He was calling on those skills now.

"Who the bloody hell are you and what the hell are you doing here?"

Unable to suppress his scream, out it came.

He recognised this woman. It was Agnes who lived in the Gate House. What the hell was he going to say now?

"You frightened the bloody life out of me!" Attack was the best form of defence (not the cubs', but his own father's advice).

"Really? For one, I live here and I am sup*posed* to be here. You, on the other hand, are not."

Think, Monty, think! He washed some excuses around his head.

"My dog appears to be in here somewhere, but I can neither find him nor hear him."

Well done, thought Monty.

"I'd like to know how he got in – there's a cattle grid at both gates," was the rather curt response.

"I didn't have to cross a cattle grid when I followed him through the hole in the hedge."

Right back at you, bitch! Although he had to admit she had a very kind face.

"What's its name?"

"I'm sorry?" *Think, Monty – again!*

"Your dog; what's its name?"

"Mavis," he replied, suddenly remembering he'd said it was a he.

"Odd name for a dog."

Great, she hasn't noticed my faux pas.

"Mmm, I expect you're right, but I didn't name her. My relative named her after her late grandmother."

OK, Monty, no need for the detail. He knew how to make something totally believable, but it really wasn't necessary here.

"Mavis, Mavis," he called out feebly. Why bother raising his voice? Mavis was never coming home.

They stood together. Neither one knew what the other expected them to do.

"Let me get my coat." Agnes felt that she should help.

Oh, bloody hell!" thought Monty. *Now there'll be two of us looking for a dog that doesn't exist.*

"What colour is she?" Agnes was building up a picture of this covert canine.

"Erm, she's brown – ish. A little bit of white on her ear."

"Breed?"

Stop with the questions. I'm all out of doggie descriptions.

Agnes was putting on her coat. They walked together shouting for 'Mavis'. Monty was desperately trying to remember where the tunnel exit was, which may expose Jordan.

Fifteen pointless minutes later they stopped looking for this bloody dog. Finally, Agnes concluded that maybe she had found her way back through the hedge and had gone home herself.

Purely just to get away from this new mess, Monty agreed. Agnes then walked him to the side gate beside the cattle grid.

Finally, he was on the road once Agnes was safely out of sight. What kind of sleuth was he exactly? He now had to go right back to the point he was originally at when he was found by Agnes.

Once again, he found himself weaving through the hedge. This time, forgoing his socks – he could feel every midge and mini fly biting him, sucking he life out of him. Hopefully they'd have drained him of any life before he reached the exact same spot he'd just been standing on.

Retracing all of his steps, he decided he'd take more notice of the house this time. Could he see anyone in there?

Aha! There she was! Agnes was in the front room with the handyman from the Hall.

Thank the dear Lord for that. He was free to roam.

Just as he was about to step out of the darkness, a figure walked right in front of him.

What the absolute hell? Who the hell can this be? He had thought this, but, in truth, he had wanted to shout it out.

He felt the person stop right in front of him. Now he could see the silhouette against the light of the room.

They were standing watching Agnes and the young man. Watching them laughing, eating some kind of cake. Generally looking like they were having fun.

Turning on itself, the figure walked into the Gate House. Initially, Monty had thought that if this was their man, he should get in there too. Three against one. What great odds and he wouldn't have to deal with it alone.

Flora walked into the room and, within minutes, they were all laughing.

What a fool he could have made of himself.

Now, anything else?

Actually, there was. Some*thing* else, that is. Monty had forgotten just how stiff this particular door was to open. It wasn't really a door, more of a lid. A lid that, in reality, didn't look like it wished to be opened again.

He pulled, nothing.

He pulled again. Still nothing.

He decided that his body was required to find the hidden strength that he hadn't ever found in himself before. It was obviously well hidden.

Apparently, that strength just wasn't there. This door was not going to budge and he would bet anyone that it wasn't going to budge for them either.

OK, he was going to have to go down Jordan's tunnel – if he could find it, that was.

Retracing his steps, Monty was beginning to feel quite at home here in the darkness.

"Yes, there it is," he announced to himself out loud. He could only see the area he was convinced was where the tunnel entrance was.

Just as he was beginning to move closer, he heard voices. Sure, it would be the friendlies in the Gate House. He was almost not that careful to remain hidden – he had an excuse after all. The dog, again, on the loose. His imagination wasn't allowed to go that far, unfortunately. The two figures that appeared against the moonlight were not who he had thought they were.

At that moment, Monty wanted to check that he was hidden enough so as not to blow his cover.

"Lock it. There's no way out for them then. They won't know about the other entrance, so if we lock that too they can stay in there tonight and we can deal with them tomorrow. Is the old bat still in the horsebox?"

"Yes, and she won't be heard no matter how loud she screams. She actually had a cosh. Surprised she could lift it. How old do you reckon she is?"

"Got to be well into her 90s. Did you see the wrinkles on her legs? Explaining what happened to her will be easy; it's these two that'll be the problem. What do we do with them?"

"Dunno; need to think this one through."

"Do we go back inside? Do we meet at the usual place? What's the plan?"

Well, these were clearly not members of the household speaking like that. Who says 'dunno' anymore? No, no. They were certainly part of the team, but what team? They had to be involved with someone in the Hall, otherwise how could they know about the tunnels? They certainly knew how to get around the place.

Monty couldn't open Jordan's lid either. He had decided someone was on to them as both lids were locked so no-one could get out.

Monty had to warn the others. He needed to get to them before these two heavies did.

As they made their way towards the Hall, Monty found himself running at great speed towards the stable yard to find the only door enabling them an exit.

Now, for the hidden strength Monty had failed to uncover from within, speed was the one thing he knew he did have. He had few fond memories, if any at all, of his boarding school days; however, when all his friends would go home for the holidays, Monty would use this time out on the athletics track or, when it was too cold (who likes outdoor sport when it's cold?) he would be allowed to use the indoor running track.

Right now, his hard work was to pay off. Never believing he would ever make Team GB, he just loved to run.

And like the wind he went – the opposite side of the Hall to The Baddies.

In what seemed like no time, he was there. Running towards the door, he could see the key hanging from the wall hook, just as it had on that first night. Nerves doing their job, he fumbled to take the key from the wall, dropping it into the straw base.

Hearing voices – familiar voices – he sees the key. Picking it up, he has a decision to make and quickly.

Where does he hide?

Finding what would be, to most people, the obvious pile of hay in one corner, he dives in.

He mostly felt comfortable here because no-one was actually looking for him and, in truth, he much preferred being covered in hay than fish shit.

The odd thing about hiding when you are not even being hunted is, as Monty felt, that your body doesn't actually recognise this fact and begins to shake impulsively. Deciding they'd just think it was a rat if they even noticed, he remained as still as his nerves would permit.

One thought that did flash through his mind was that he had two incredible fears in his life; one was the fear of being eaten by a shark, the other was accidentally touching a rat and, right now, of those two possibilities, one was a very real and highly probable threat. He prayed silently that the two idiots would realise their plan couldn't work and leave, allowing him his release as rat bait.

He began to sweat.

"Where's the key?" asked Man A (Monty had named them in the most basic fashion).

"I didn't check where it was; where is it usually?" enquired Man B.

"No idea. We'll wedge that chair against the handle, that'll work just as well. It's only till tomorrow."

"What happens to Granny?"

"She stays put until we've seen the Boss. He wants to see us in the pub. He wants us to be seen."

With that, they were gone.

Counting to 20 (30 would have been better, but he knew he wouldn't get that far without screaming out loud), Monty removed himself from his hell of hay and brushed himself off.

He needed to act fast. Not only did he need to find the other two, they had to get Auntie Mildred out of the horsebox and there were a few of them.

Removing the chair (how amateur), he decided to use his gadget given to him by Jordan and proceeded to send a text to them both telling them to make their way to the doorway. It was at this point that Beth responded with questions.

No questions Beth. Just get here.

Monty I have no idea how to get there. I'll
go back to the opening. Of course, Jordan had
entered via another tunnel.

They've locked the lid Jordan. You're going to
have to find a way out. They have Auntie and they
are coming back for her and the two of you. We
don't have much time.

Monty decided it best not to go through the door, just in case they
came back and saw the door had been opened. Instead, he stood
behind the main door with the chair, which he decided to use as a
club if needed.

Literally five minutes later, Beth came hurtling through the
door.

"What the hell has happened, Monty, and how do you know
all of this?" Beth was sweaty and full of dust, but she seemed to
understand not to wait for a response to her question.

"Do we go to find Auntie Mildred?" she asked. Knowing
Jordan, he'd get out somehow. Right now, and pressed for time,
they decided to text him to tell him what they were doing and then
they both made their way to the variety of horseboxes.

"It looks like a car park at the Horse of the fucking Year Show!"
Monty was beyond despair.

"OK, Monty, you start at one end and me the other. If she is in a
box, she'll be in the back, so don't bother with the doors in the cab,
try the small door at the back of each box."

Off they went to find their old friend who was probably
dehydrated and frightened to death by now.

Fifteen minutes had passed. Nothing from Jordan, but Beth had
to put him to the back of her mind right now; he was resourceful
beyond belief so he would find a way out, she knew it.

It was Beth who found her. As soon as she climbed into this
particular box, it wasn't instantly obvious it was Auntie Mildred.

Beth found a pair of Pretty Polly tights wrapped around her head and neck.

"Auntie Mildred," Beth said, speaking as quietly as she could, not wanting to cause her any more alarm.

Auntie Mildred realised pretty quickly who her visitor was. Relief spread across her face as much as the Pretty Polly tights would allow.

Beth whispered into her ear.

"Don't say a word, Auntie Mildred, just follow me."

Texting Monty, he joined them both in seconds and, for the first time in his life, he expressed his emotions towards his auntie.

"Yes, yes, I'm alive. Monty, I'm OK."

Unable to release his vice-like grip, Auntie Mildred peeled his fingers from her arms.

"Enough. I'm not good with fuss; let's get the hell out of here."

"Have you heard from Jordan, Beth?" Monty's concern was now for his other friend.

"No, nothing." Beth was solely focused on her husband now. At the same time, she realised they couldn't possibly stay here. They had to make their way towards the Gate House and work out how they could get Auntie Mildred out unnoticed for she could hardly crawl through the hedge.

It didn't seem to take them long to get to the trees.

They all looked into the Gate House. Standing as handsome as hell in the kitchen was Jordan.

Whispering, Beth told them both to follow her. She took them both to the gap in the hedge.

Now she felt she could talk.

"Auntie Mildred, there is no way you can get through here, so I'm going to go to the house and get some clippers to try and create a bit more height, so you can crouch and get through easier."

"No time for that, Beth," and with that, Auntie Mildred was straight on the floor and through the hole all of them had struggled with in some way.

Once they were all safely through, they made their way to the house as discreetly as they could.

At home, they all changed, very quickly. Beth picked up her bag, purse and car keys.

She'd give Jordan 15 minutes, then she'd go to the Gate House.

As soon as Jordan knew his exit was closed off, he searched for another route, which he found quite easily – certainly easier than he'd anticipated. He didn't need to walk too far before he found another set of steps leading him to the surface. This time he came out right by the front gates, literally right beside the cattle grid, but you would never have found it under normal circumstances.

Fresh air, at last. As he stood for what seemed like a minute or two, he heard a female voice.

"Don't tell me, you've lost your dog?"

It was Agnes.

CHAPTER TWELVE

"My dog, yes, I've lost it; how did you know?"

"Your friend, he was on the hunt earlier. He thought she might have gone home. Poor Mavis. What breed is she; your friend didn't say?"

Mavis – only Monty could come up with a name like that. Not Growler or Satan to ward anyone off. No, it had to be Mavis, Jordan thought.

"Breed? Oh, she's quite small. To be honest, she isn't mine so I wouldn't know. Mongrel, I think."

"Oh, I hope you find her."

"Hey Jordan, what's up?" Now Flora was on the scene.

"Hiya Flora. It's Auntie Mildred's dog; she's gone missing."

"I didn't realise she had a dog; I didn't see her when I came round."

Bloody hell, Monty!

"Oh, she's quite old and a bit incontinent, so Auntie Mildred keeps her in the utility room. Bloody dog."

"Oh, I hope she hasn't been taken by a fox."

I bloody hope she has, thought Jordan. *That would put an end to this ridiculous storyline.*

"Why don't you come in to warm up?" suggested Flora.

Jordan didn't want to go in. He wanted to go and help his wife. He knew she would know he would be OK, but even so, he wanted to make sure *she* was OK. Auntie Mildred was an old lady and this was a serious situation.

Perhaps he would go in for five minutes, then go home. At least he'd shown his face.

Inside the Gate House, Jordan was suddenly reminded of his childhood. Those smells of home cooking – not something he was familiar with in his own home. Poor Beth, she would bake a cake and you only ever heard of the success stories. Those were in short supply. The failures, when he was home, he would find in the garden for the birds.

Beth was more the baker and he the chef.

He had been taught by his mother. Spices, herbs and oils.

Beth had learned something different during her childhood – love – and that was certainly not in short supply.

"Thanks for the tea. It's been a while since I've had tea from a pot! Thanks for the cake too. Very nice." Jordan was directing this to the young man whose name he didn't quite catch but, nonetheless, he was lovely and Jordan could see he was devoted to Flora. Funny though, she didn't mention she had a boyfriend when she came round.

"Let me show you out," said Agnes, "there's an access gate beside the cattle grid. I think it would be lovely for all of you to come over for dinner one evening. Let me know and I'll organise it. It would be lovely to do it before you all go home."

As Jordan walked away from her, his desire to run like the clappers was so great, but he couldn't let them see that.

How hilarious. This was their home. The fixes they'd gotten themselves into during this past couple of weeks. A dog they haven't got, a house they own, but it's thought that Auntie Mildred has just moved in. What next?

He was running now.

Suddenly he was aware of a car driving towards him, flashing its lights.

Sitting at the wheel was Beth. She was alone. His heart sank. Pulling up, he jumped in.

Beth could never credit herself with a standard three-point turn. Typically, she would make such a meal of it. Not tonight.

With Jordan barely able to say a word, within seconds they were belting in the opposite direction towards their house.

"What's happened, Beth?"

"Let's just get to the others, they're in the house but they can't stay there – *we* can't stay there tonight."

Pulling up onto the drive, Jordan was instantly able to see the heads of both Monty and Auntie Mildred. Curtains wrapped around each head. Monty above Auntie Mildred.

"They've obviously never read up on how to spy discreetly." Beth was quite alarmed by their utter lack of understanding about this situation.

"For god's sake, you two! The whole village can see you. Every light in the house is on and you're both peering out of the window like two targets at the fair."

They sat in the snug. It was small and darkness filled the room other than the candle in the fireplace.

Beth relayed what had happened to them all.

Jordan did the same.

"OK, this is what we do," began Monty.

"We go to the Gate House. We tell them what's happened from day one until now. We stay right under the nose of the killer. No-one will look for us there. I think this is the only option right now"

"Hang on." Beth was a little alarmed at the thought they would be involving others. This needed to be as tight as possible. How did they know they wouldn't go right to the police? This would cause a problem for them not having involved them earlier. Beth found herself saying this out loud.

"We don't know, Beth; however, as soon as they realise Auntie Mildred isn't in that horsebox, they will realise equally as quickly that we are not in those tunnels and, if I were them I'd be coming right to this house. I think we need to leave and we need to do that right now and, by the way, we will be walking there. The car stays here. We've all got two minutes to grab a bag and a few essentials and then we go."

No-one argued with him.

The challenge of choosing a few essentials was quite an easy one for Monty. He had ruined so many of his things; he put some pants, socks, jeans (ugh), shirt, jumper and toiletries into his bag and was downstairs first.

Jordan was next; he'd barely unpacked, so everything was to hand. Bag packed, he spent the remaining minute checking all the doors were locked and the curtains were closed. Alarm ready to be engaged.

Beth was pretty low maintenance. She always had a bag prepared with spare clothes and toiletries so she simply threw in her make-up essentials. Even sleuths needed to look good.

Auntie Mildred had packed very quickly – she was now looking for random things in her room that could double up as a weapon. A comb with a long, thin, metal stem. Three glass balls with a flower inside each one. A pair of nail scissors. These would do and surely the others would be thinking along the same lines.

Once they were all downstairs, Beth took a quick look to check the coast was clear and ushered them outside, leaving Jordan to set the alarm.

They walked slowly along the grass edge to the Hall. Under normal circumstances, this would be hilarious. They looked like schoolkids out on a day trip. Single file, each holding the hand of the person in front of them.

Reaching the Gate House, both Jordan and Monty immediately went to open the gate to the side of the cattle grid.

Looking at each other, Jordan said, "The dog story exit?"

They smiled at each other. There was, however, little time right now for humour.

Knocking on the door to the Gate House, it was Flora who opened up.

"Hi, oh hi everyone." She was suddenly aware that there were multiple people at her door. It was also as dark as hell so she assumed the other three with Monty would be the family.

"Do come in. Is everything OK?"

"No, it's not," replied Beth, aware that Agnes and Frank were now standing in the hallway too.

Beth looked at the three completely bewildered faces staring right back at her.

"Can you please lock all doors in the house and close all of the windows. We will stay in here as it's concealed. Please do this and we will explain what's going on."

Beth was not questioned. The three rushed around the house closing curtains and locking doors. This was easy; it was just the front door and the back door.

"OK," announced Agnes, "all done. Can you please let us know what the hell is going on because you are beginning to frighten me."

They sat in the kitchen. This was a little risky due to the fact it was quite an exposed room in the sense that there were many windows. If they should be talking in anything above a whisper and someone was standing the other side of the wall, they would, at the very least, expose themselves. That said, no-one was looking for them.

"Don't worry about the windows," said Flora who noticed Beth looking around the room. "They not only have curtains, they have blinds too. Agnes says it's always cold in here, so she doubled up on draught exclusion."

Beth began the history of events, starting with an explanation as to the ownership of their house and her relationship with Auntie Mildred and Monty.

As she relayed the story, everyone, including Beth, struggled to make sense of it all.

Much of what was said brought horror to the faces of their three new confidants.

It took Beth half an hour or so to recall everything and two strong cups of coffee. Auntie Mildred and Monty chose wine. The whole experience brought on emotions only wine could temper.

"Hang on." It was Flora who delved in first to try and further understand their story. "You said you had a delivery of fish guts in a bin plonked on your driveway, didn't you?"

"That's right," confirmed Beth. "Why?"

"Because the stable yard at the Hall had a horrible stench of fish during the week. I asked where it was coming from, but the staff around there didn't know. I asked you; do you remember, Agnes? I wondered if it was something that had gone off in the kitchen."

"Yes," replied Agnes, "it *was* awful, but the source couldn't be found."

"Well, that would tie in with someone from the Hall having some knowledge at least of this chain of events," said Monty.

"I can't believe anyone died that night. How could they and yet no-one be reported missing? It doesn't make sense," said Frank.

"The night of the event in the Hall, there were tons of people there. Some were local but others came from all over the place." Agnes was trying to remain positive. "Even though the invites were far and wide, if someone didn't go home, that would make the news, wouldn't it?"

"I would expect so," said Jordan, "but not unless it was someone who had no-one to go home *to*. It's possible they wouldn't have been reported yet."

That wasn't a likely outcome, but was quite possible.

"Sorry to remind you of this, but what about the finger?" Monty hadn't wanted to remind himself of this but it was, after all, a rather noteworthy piece of information.

"A finger?" was the unison response from Agnes, Flora and Frank.

"Oh shit, I forgot about that." Beth couldn't believe she had missed this out.

"Yes," she said, "we felt that changed things. That's why we wanted to get back to the original room to see if there was anything else so that we could go to the police with something substantial."

"I think," Flora was standing up now, "we need to get back to that room so I can try to figure out which room in the Hall is above it. The Hall is huge and there are many rooms that I haven't even been in."

Beth and co couldn't believe anyone could live in a house that was so big that there were rooms they hadn't ever been in. How odd.

"I am absolutely not leaving this house. I'm lucky my heart still has any kind of beat." Auntie Mildred was happy holding her comfort blanket disguised as an almost empty bottle of wine. She wasn't prepared to leave this house for anything or anyone. No, she would stay here until this whole business was resolved. There seemed to be enough booze to tide her over. She'd worked that out within minutes of being here.

Monty had tried, twice, to prise the bottle from her vice-like grip in order to fill up his glass.

Selfish cow, he thought to himself. Without thinking, he stood up and grabbed another bottle. His manners left at the gate, he felt entitled to drink whatever he wished.

"I wouldn't let you leave this house." Agnes looked at this old lady. How had she survived this entire series of events? To think that she actually came back to beef up the numbers of this most unlikely team of investigators.

"Frank, I think you should stay here with Mildred. You know the outside of the Hall like no-one else, but the inside – well, that's Flora and I. We need you, Monty and Beth because you know the room and, Jordan, you are the tour de force."

Everyone agreed with this distribution of resources.

Agnes and Flora went upstairs to get changed.

As she gathered her outdoor wear, Agnes felt a sudden rush of excitement. Recognising this wasn't a trip to the funfair, more a very dangerous evening's work ahead, she still felt the adrenaline increasing throughout her body. Did she have anything she could use to protect them from certain danger? The answer was no. Not unless she took a kitchen knife. *That would be a bad idea*, she thought. Hearing what she had just now, the wrong person would undoubtedly get stabbed. There was too much that had gone wrong for the right person to be the recipient of a knife wound. No, she would leave the knives in the kitchen.

Flora, however, once dressed in her combat gear, had a whole host of things she could distribute for protective purposes.

Pepper spray – this had been given to her by her mother (illegally) but for justifiable purposes should she encounter anyone as she went to her car following a late shift. A mallet – she found this in the yard and decided she would keep it – who could have known?

Picking up several syringes (all of them empty), they were light and, once you'd taken off the plastic protection, could offer short-term assistance in buying them a few seconds to escape.

Flora, too, felt the adrenaline building up. Her life was quite dull when she was at home. This felt a little like a red phone call in Resus at work. You know it's going to be bad and you need to act quickly. This was no different; she could feel it.

Monty, who had hoped he could stay in the house with Auntie Mildred, felt sick at the thought he had to go back down there. He was having all kinds of conversations with himself.

You're an adult, say no. Tell them you're not going. Tell them you've been drinking; you haven't got a clear head. You're an independent man with a mind of your own. You make your own decisions.

"Ready, Monty?" Beth put her arm around his shoulders almost aware of what battle was going on in his head.

"Yep," he replied.

For all his arguments and all of them justifiable, he knew he needed to see this out to the end. Come what may, he had to do this. Also, he could talk about his experience in his daily write-ups for weeks if not months to come. He knew he wrote well and he would have much to write about. There was plenty of meat on this bone. The angles he could explore and exploit. Oh yes. Suddenly, he too felt that ripple of excitement.

And so, they stood in the kitchen, all ready to go. Each with their own thoughts, but all united in the journey that lay ahead.

No-one had noticed that Beth had taken the gas hob lighter from the side table. Just in case.

CHAPTER THIRTEEN

Bad guys always feel they have the upper hand. They base this on them holding the fear card. The one thing they can never accept is someone outsmarting them.

As soon as they reached the horsebox and found it empty, anger filled their veins. This was not good.

"Where is she?"

"No idea; how could she have got out of here? She must have had help."

What they couldn't understand was that no-one could have known where she was. They went straight to the stable yard and into the barn.

There was their answer.

Door open, chair by the entrance to the main door.

She had indeed had help.

Yet, how the hell could someone have known? The others were down in the tunnels. None of this made sense.

OK, now they had a problem. They had to get to her house and quick. They would certainly call the cops.

Running to their car, they were hurtling up the drive so quickly.

"I think you should slow down. If you go past the Gate House at this speed, they'll wonder what's going on. It'll invite unwanted attention."

That made sense. The driver did slow down considerably.

The thing you need to be in situations like this is alert. Tiredness usually takes this away, but tonight, our team seemed more alert than ever.

Weaving their way through the trees, Flora was the first to see the lights of the car. They stopped immediately. The vehicle went past them and away a little in the distance, but they decided this was nothing to do with them. They were driving way too slow.

The car turned left towards their home. Jordan was less convinced.

"We need to get a move on. Let's not assume anything. If that car had our potential captors inside, it won't be long before it comes back. I reckon we've got about ten minutes to get into the tunnel."

Everyone picked up their pace. Monty was wishing he'd had less wine; still, at least it masked the horror of their situation.

Auntie Mildred had Frank were re-living his childhood and how he came to be at the Hall. It was with a degree of envy that she listened to the amazing relationship he had with Agnes and what he had with her late husband. Auntie Mildred decided then and there that she would make more of an effort to show Monty some affection. That had always been lacking in their relationship. Loving him like her own son, she decided that the sins of her past should not dictate her relationship with her nephew, although, she had to admit, at times, he did drive her mad and she wondered which of the two turned the other to the wine bottle. In truth, neither needed to use the other as an excuse, they both loved a glass or two. What was the saying? 'If you can't have one at eleven, have eleven at one.' Auntie Mildred smiled. Lovely Monty. Her nephew and her friend. He would do anything for her. She did very little for him, *However,* she thought, *this may now be that time.*

The entire time that Frank was talking to her, she was drawn to a rug on the kitchen floor.

"What an odd place for a rug," observed Auntie Mildred.

"Yes, not sure why it's there – I think Lady Grey gave it to Agnes and she felt she needed to keep it in the house. I don't think she likes it very much. We all trip over it most days."

Auntie Mildred decided she'd take a look. Rugs in kitchens are usually *under* tables; they aren't often positioned where this one was.

As she lifted up the rug, she looked immediately at Frank (mostly for his reaction), which, in truth, was as curious as her own.

Lying beneath the rug was what looked like a manhole covered in the same tiles as the rest of the kitchen floor.

At one end of the manhole was a ring rather like the one you'd see on a bull's nose, but bigger.

"What the hell is under there?" Auntie Mildred knew instantly that her quiet night in this safe house under the protection of her recently appointed bodyguard was just about to change.

Frank, who'd had no experience of drama other than Dutch elm or slug issues, would have to learn pretty quickly.

Auntie Mildred bent forward to try to open the lid.

"You can't do that, Mildred. Let me."

Frank pulled on the ring. Apprehension being his number one priority here. If any of what they'd relayed earlier was true, something told him that with only Mildred on his side, he had every reason to close the lid and pretend they'd never found it. Something else told him Mildred would not allow that to happen.

The lid, with one full twist, opened with relative ease. How could Agnes not know this was there? If she *did* know, why had she never mentioned it before?

It was like staring into blackness. There is an odd thing about blackness; you can convince yourself that it's quite welcoming.

"I'll get my torch." Auntie Mildred delved into her pockets.

"Resourceful, aren't you?" Frank was quite surprised. This old lady was quite something. You would have thought she was decades younger than her actual years.

Shining the torch into the blackness, the only thing it revealed was a set of steps. These steps were the most uninviting-looking, not to mention the most incredibly unsafe steps either of them had ever seen.

"Let me go first, Mildred. They don't look safe. We don't even know how deep they go."

Auntie Mildred offered no resistance to his suggestion.

His descent was not actually that unsafe. The steps looked far less robust than they felt.

He counted 20 steps. The light had faded from the torch, but he was still able to see the floor, which was literally just earth. It had the same smell as the beds in the garden.

Auntie Mildred was careful not to close the lid; this was most likely their exit as much as their entrance.

"I'm on my way. What's at the bottom?"

"I can't see. Take your time. We can figure it out when you're down here."

Mildred is quite agile, thought Frank. It didn't seem to take her as long to get down as it had him.

Reaching the bottom, Frank found himself asking the obvious question.

"Mildred, why are we coming down here? We don't have to be here."

"No, you are quite right, Frank, we don't have to be here. We *need* to be here. You see, your family and mine are putting themselves at great risk. They are likely to be found by these awful people. We are technically *not* here. We are also at the other side of the Hall. The action is a good way off. The least we can do is try to find an alternative way out for them."

Frank said nothing more and, by the light of the tiny torch, they could see there was only one direction they could proceed.

Frank decided he should go first. If anyone was going to come up against trouble, it should really be him.

"Here." Auntie Mildred offered him the torch and a pair of tights weighted down with something.

"It's a homemade cosh. The first one I made served me well."

At the house, the men walked around. They checked all doors, which were predictably locked.

Curtains closed. This could be a ploy to make them think they were all in bed when they were, in fact, lying in wait. The police could be in there too. It was far too risky. They couldn't go in.

One man put his hand on the bonnet of the car.

"This is still warm."

"Then wherever they have gone, they have gone on foot if they aren't in the house."

Leaving one man at the house, the other two decided they'd

return to the Hall. They had the space to think there.

"Did you see them on the road as we came back from the pub? I didn't."

"No, but there are two ways down this road. They may have walked the other way."

They decided they would take a drive in the opposite direction just to see if they could see anyone.

Nothing and no-one.

Turning back, neither of the men really knew what they would do next.

As they dealt with their confusion in one part of the village, Monty and co continued on as planned in another.

Reaching the barn, the first thing Monty noticed was the chair, which had been moved from the front door. It was now positioned in a corner with a bucket on top of it.

"They've been back in here." He explained how he knew that.

"Then we have to get through that door and into the tunnel network. Don't touch anything we don't have to touch. If they come back, which I expect they will, they can't think anyone has been here since they were last here." Beth's mind was racing.

All processed through the door, two of them not having a clue what to expect, but for the other three, this now seemed like familiar territory.

The route was an easy one; there was only one way to go. All of a sudden, Beth saw the flaw in their plan.

"How do we get out of here? If we go back, we will undoubtedly walk right into them. From here we don't know where we are going."

"Our job is to get to the room. We need to know which room sits above it so Agnes and Flora stand a chance of finding it inside the house."

The order was Beth, Agnes, Flora, Jordan and then Monty taking up the rear.

Why am I going last? I'm actually the most scared out of us all. I've seen films with scenes like this. It's always the one who is in the last position who gets it first. Of course, he would have been a fool to say these words out loud.

He was genuinely scared to death. They should have discussed their positioning. He would never have put himself in last place.

Jordan, who had less faith in the constitution of their friend, asked if he would like to swap places. Monty didn't reply; he simply pushed past Jordan, instantly feeling a sense of protection – a nurse in front and a beefcake behind – the perfect sandwich right now.

It seemed as though they had been walking for an hour when in fact it had barely been five minutes.

"Not too much further now." Beth felt the need to reassure everyone.

Pretty soon after they stood beneath the floorboards that had once borne the weight of the poor man whose current state of life or death remained unknown.

"Everyone needs to whisper," Beth had whispered. "I think we should stand in a circle and speak only if there is something we see or we think is relevant." These had been the very clear instructions Beth had given prior to going inside the tunnel.

The room above was lit. It hadn't been that night. The cracks in the boards offered just enough light for them to scour the room.

Nothing. Absolutely not a single thing that they could take back with them.

Flora was on her toes, trying to see anything through the cracks, anything that would give her an idea of the room they were beneath. She was sure though that she had never been in this room.

Agnes, slightly smaller than Flora and who was also on her toes, did wonder if she herself had been in there. Were they books in a pile on the floor? It was hopeless; they should have brought the chair with them. They could have stood on that.

That was it – the chair. Someone had to go back for the chair.

"I've had an idea. We need that chair from the stable barn. We can stand on it to see a bit more of the room. There's definitely a rug over a large part of the floor – maybe we could cut a little piece and then go round the rooms to see which one it's from."

"That is a very bad idea, Agnes. Firstly, if we head back, we could bump into them. If we make it to the barn and take the chair they will know we've been in there." Monty was ready for the fight on this one just in case they suggested it was he who should go.

"Does someone want to get on my shoulders? I could lift you up." Jordan could see no reason why this couldn't achieve the same outcome.

"It should be Flora," suggested Beth, "or Agnes. They will know what they are looking for or what they have seen if they go back into the Hall."

Flora climbed onto Jordan's shoulders and, as he rose, she could see quite clearly that this was a totally unfamiliar room to her.

Suddenly, they heard voices above them. *Not for the first time,* thought Beth and Monty.

"You have got to be joking. Are you both idiots? How can a fragile, old woman get away from you? You must be joking. How do we know the police are not going to be here in the next couple of minutes? I'm not paying you for this. No deal. You didn't scare her, you didn't kill her and you couldn't contain her in a fucking horsebox. So, what are you suggesting? And this had better be good."

"We locked the doors to the tunnels, but they got out."

"This just gets worse. How the hell did they get out?"

"Dunno. Is there another way in?"

"There are many ways into that network. They would have to know about them though."

Flora froze. The others too were motionless. Looking down to the others, she raised her hands and shook her head.

Who were these men in her home? She didn't recognise a single voice. Her family must know them or were they holding her parents and her brother hostages? Oh, this was all too much.

Suddenly, she felt quite light-headed. She couldn't see anyone, she recognised nothing. She looked straight at Agnes who, to Ruth, looked very worried indeed. Did she know these people? If she did, why didn't she recognise them herself? They seemed to be pretty comfortable in her house. Her mother would certainly never approve of these types of people in her home. As she lifted her head up again to try and see any of the faces, she felt so light-headed. Moving her arms to steady herself, she inadvertently smacked Monty on the side of his face.

In that moment, and forgetting his whereabouts, Monty let out a whimper; albeit a relatively quiet sound, it was enough to bring the meeting upstairs to an abrupt end.

No-one upstairs said a word. Everyone downstairs froze once more, but this time, they moved to the side of the room just in case someone peered through the gaps.

It was quite remarkable how this group of people, out of their depth and filled with fear, knew that every single move they made had to be hushed. They managed to navigate themselves through the darkness in absolute silence.

Monty, forgetting in an instant all his fears, felt it was his responsibility to buy them a little time to work out what they could do.

He would still go out for a run, just as he used to around the old sports field at school. He still had it, or something similar.

It was in that moment in the room that Monty remembered he still had the key to the door. If he locked it, they wouldn't be able to access through there. This would buy them a little more time to figure something out.

Once he had run there, he raced for the chair, but why? He had no clue.

Closing the door behind him, then locking it. Checking it, then checking it again.

Back he ran.

As soon as he was in the room he gathered everyone together and whispered what he had done.

"That's bloody brilliant," whispered Jordan.

"I'm so sorry everyone." Flora was devastated. Her actions could cost them dearly. Likening this to her job, poor decisions and badly timed accidents could cost lives. This was no different.

"We think they are still up there," whispered Beth, "as we haven't heard anyone leave yet."

Very carefully, Jordan felt his way around the room for a door in any of the walls.

Nothing.

Then, as he felt the floor in the room, it wasn't so much as a trapdoor that he felt, it was more of a shallow dip. When he felt around a little more, he could feel some kind of carpet.

He stood up. He knew what was under there.

"OK, everyone, we need to get out of here. There is no exit other than the door over there. I can't believe that between here and the barn, there is no other spike off into another tunnel."

Jordan's mining experience taught him that networks of tunnels, whilst complicated, were usually created to lead somewhere, so to have dug a tunnel such as this for it to lead to just one room didn't make sense.

Now that he knew what he was sure he knew, this was no longer a dangerous situation; it had possibilities of becoming something a little more sinister. This was murder and if they could kill once, they could certainly do it again.

At least those in this tunnel were quite agile – Auntie Mildred would have been a liability right now. He knew they needed to move quickly.

Beth, who could read her husband's face, could see he wasn't happy. It was gloomy and hard to tell, but she was sure this was very bad whatever it was. What could possibly have caused this sudden change to his attitude? They were all aware of the dangers when they came down here.

Monty's state of mind was likened to Red Alert the minute they decided they had to come down here. He had an awful feeling running through him. He felt a sudden need to pee. That was obviously out of the question. Ladies' and gents' amenities seemed to be in short supply. He didn't want to be the kid in the back seat of the car going on holiday who needed a wee 10 minutes in. No, he would have to wait. Think of something else.

Actually, it was that something else that was giving him the urge.

"We need to feel around the wall, look for a door."

Everyone began to feel their way around. Suddenly, there was a light. Everyone but Monty froze.

"Monty! What the absolute hell!" Beth was in disbelief.

"What?" Monty had no idea why he was being targeted.

"You have a torch!" Now Jordan was pissed off.

"Yes, I've always had it. You gave it to me, Jordan; it's the one that doesn't reflect too far."

"Please may I have it?" Beth just took it from him and handed it to Jordan who, as quick as the flash that Monty wasn't, skimmed the tunnel for some kind of exit door.

And there it was.

It wasn't really a door; it was literally a very thin slit in the wall with a ring that he twisted. The gap opened up quite nicely into another dark alley. They all filed in.

Flora and Agnes had said hardly anything since the men upstairs had been around. Neither of them knew what was going on. Flora couldn't believe she was actually in the grounds of her own home and Agnes couldn't believe the goings-on that had probably occurred all the years she'd lived here. It felt as though they were in some kind of very, very bad nightmare.

Beth took the rear of the group. She felt it was only right since Monty had assumed this position (reluctantly) each time. In truth, Monty had wanted the rear position just in case he needed to go. *How odd*, he thought to himself, *here we are in the middle of an escape from probable murderers and all I can think of right now is my bladder.*

Not knowing what was above them, there were no floorboards here, but given the proximity of 'the room' above, they assumed there could still be a chance that they could be heard if they were to speak in anything above a whisper.

They moved slowly yet with purpose. Jordan was able to use the torch; he felt confident enough that the light wasn't going to give away their presence. This tunnel was much narrower than the other one had been and both the previous ones. There seemed to be a bend but he was so disorientated he didn't bother to think about where they could be heading.

On they went for what seemed like an age.

Monty would definitely need to pee, but how could he get

around this in such a way that no-one would notice?

Certain of one thing, it had to happen. He decided to allow the other two to pass him by and he would discreetly swap places with Beth.

Beth was far too highly charged to wonder why he'd suggested the shift in their order; she simply took his place and followed the others.

Within moments, Monty was back behind Beth.

"Where did you go?"

"Nature called."

"Nature – well, that's the last word I expected to hear down here," Beth smiled. *It must be nerves*, thought Beth. *Monty would never do anything like that, let alone admit to it.*

Jordan thought he saw something further ahead; it looked a little like another door, but didn't want to raise any hopes.

He was right. It seemed to Jordan that the further they went inside this maze, the less they seemed to have cared about the doorways.

"OK, guys, here's another door. As with the last one, let's stay on our toes and be as quiet as we can be."

"Before we go in," piped up Monty, "does anyone else feel like we are on *I'm a Celebrity…*?"

"Sorry, no." Flora's anxiety was becoming overbearing and Beth quietly assumed she'd probably never watched it or didn't know what it was.

Agnes sensed this and touched her shoulder. She had to admit that Monty had a point and she would recall this feeling later. Not too sure why she felt things would be OK for them, but she did, and that would certainly be a line to remember.

Jordan pressed his head against the (let's call it a barrier). A door would look quite different.

He heard nothing coming from the other side, so decided he would take a chance and go through.

CHAPTER FOURTEEN

Auntie Mildred and Frank, once below the ground, were determined to find their friends. Auntie Mildred was clutching her cosh as she would typically clutch an expensive handbag. It gave her a sense of power. Secretly, she was hoping she could use it. The men responsible for all of this had caused her personal pain and fear. Usually, anyone who crossed Auntie Mildred would know about it – she had far more enemies than friends. However, this last week or so, she had hoped to turn that around.

Frank was, well, he was in complete shock. He had thought himself to be on the ball. He was aware of what was going on around him, but clearly he was blinkered and not observant at all. Flora needed him. He wanted her to know that he needed her too. How could he possibly tell someone like Flora how he felt about her? Would she think he was interested in her or her money? Surely she knew him better than that. At least he hoped she did.

Frank felt the need to take charge, but he honestly didn't think Mildred would hear of it so he allowed her to take the lead, which she did without discussion.

"Do you have any idea where this leads?" Auntie Mildred thought perhaps some kind of direction would be helpful.

"I didn't even know this web was down here so, no, I don't have any idea, unfortunately." As he said this, he thought he could see something on the ground.

Their tunnel (not that they realised the huge advantage of this) was much wider than what the others were sliding along. Frank passed Auntie Mildred and headed towards the area of interest. Frank had a torch – it was as bright as the moon on a clear night.

He also had a number of tools, which could be useful. He didn't realise he had most of them; they were work tools in the pocket of his coat.

As he reached the area, he could clearly see a lid. Reaching forward for the handle, which was, in fact, a huge ring, Auntie Mildred intervened… again.

"Let me go down first. If I am attacked or caught in any way, you have young legs and can get out of here much quicker than I could if you had gone in first."

Frank could understand the rationale behind this trail of thought, although he did worry that the bottom could be a long way down.

"OK, but first I have to look how far down the hole is. Mildred, once I have the door open, please don't say anything. We really need to be so quiet. Let's not invite trouble; we don't really know how dangerous these people are."

Auntie Mildred knew that all right!

Meanwhile, Jordan and Beth had their own issues.

Jordan shone his torch into the void. He had no idea what he was looking into; his torch was relatively dim so he would need to tread carefully.

"I think I should go in alone. Let me suss out what's in there and if there's even any point going inside."

Beth was a little annoyed that Jordan seemed to be taking over her adventure. Who made *him* the boss? He had his own mines and tunnels. This was *her* gig.

Now she was at the back of the pack and with no way of getting ahead of the others, she felt a little bit useless.

Jordan sensed that this was a very small room. Barely bigger than their kitchen at home. What was the point of this room, then? He was the only one who had seen and then felt the mound beneath the rug in the other 'holding room'. Before then, there was no real evidence that there had even been a murder – no body – no real evidence of anything, but this changed a short while ago. He didn't want to tell the others because he didn't see how that would be helpful right now.

As he turned his back towards the door, he heard a rustling above his head. Immediately, he turned off his torch. He had nothing really to use as a weapon. Nothing but his bare hands and, thankfully, a pretty decent punch, at least that's how it felt when someone tried to steal his briefcase in Australia last year. A middle-aged, very unassuming chap, quick as you like, grabbed the handle and walked off as though he'd had it in his hand all along. Jordan remembered seeing him walk away. As he stood to touch the guy's shoulder, he turned around and pushed Jordan in the face with his own briefcase. One punch back and he knocked the chap to the ground.

Yes, he had now stirred up enough emotional anger to tackle whatever was about to happen to him.

Jordan felt a waft of air across his face. This was it. He had to handle this on his own and give the others a chance to run.

Absolute pitch-black. Even though he was aware that there was an opening above, it gave nothing away.

He could hear and feel someone coming inside his room. They must have a stepladder or something.

From one dark, dank space to another.

Frank and Auntie Mildred had already discussed how she would get down there. His torch had revealed the drop wasn't too bad. Auntie Mildred would sit at the end of the ledge and he would lower her down, allowing her to slide through his arms. He'd lifted her already to assess her weight.

"Wasn't this a *Dirty Dancing* move?" Frank wasn't sure why he'd tried to crack a joke with someone who rarely smiled and who made no exception now.

Auntie Mildred literally weighed nothing. For someone who was used to bags of potatoes, equipment and trees, Auntie Mildred seemed almost weightless.

Legs dangling, with arms lifted high above her head, Frank was poised to lower her down.

Like two scenes on the same stage, acted out simultaneously.

Jordan in the very space below felt this was his time to take action. Waving his hands above him, he had a sixth sense he was about to go into battle.

Suddenly, he felt something. Instinctively, he grabbed what he could feel and pulled it.

Auntie Mildred, only expecting to be lowered gently to the ground, had the shock of her life when she felt something grab her. In the blink of an eye, she did two things: grab onto the edge of the hole and then grab her faithful friend from her pocket.

There – she was gone – pulled from their room into another. Even in the darkness, Frank felt as though an illuminated image would still look like a scene from a horror movie.

Auntie Mildred didn't have the time to get into her pocket properly; she needed her hand to steady herself, which also proved fruitless.

Both Auntie Mildred and Jordan fell to the ground, neither realising whom the other was. Thankfully, Mildred fell on top of her attacker, which gave her the time to grab her cosh.

Whack!

This guy was not getting up any time soon from that.

"Frank," she whispered.

"What the hell just happened?"

"I got him with my cosh. Get me back up."

They had not planned for this manoeuvre.

"Let me put my torch on."

"Oh fuck!" cried Auntie Mildred.

"It's Jordan – I think I've killed Jordan."

Everyone on the other side of the door heard this and raced into the room.

There stood Auntie Mildred and there lay Jordan.

"Auntie Mildred, what have you done to him?" Beth was beside herself. "Jordan, Jordan, can you hear me?"

He was breathing, at least.

"Let me see him," said Flora.

Rushing to his side, Flora immediately reverted to autopilot.

"He's going to be OK, but he will have a headache tomorrow."

Jordan, who had been out cold for around five minutes, was now coming round.

"What are you doing here, Auntie Mildred?" Monty was, once again, shaking his head.

"Is that you up there, Frank?" Flora called up as quietly as she could.

"Yep, I'm here. I think you all need to come back through here. It leads to the kitchen in the Coach House."

"What?" Agnes couldn't believe what she was hearing. A night full of shocks and surprises, all right.

"No time for this, folks." Beth was now becoming frustrated. "Let's get us all out of here."

Jordan, who had only just sat up, couldn't imagine climbing up anywhere, but he knew that he must.

He still had his secret.

Auntie Mildred climbed onto Monty's shoulders allowing Frank to lift her out and then it was Flora's turn. *She's heavier than she looks*, thought Monty.

Agnes, who Monty decided best not to judge, asked Beth if he could put his arms onto her shoulders. Hopefully this would give him a little more strength to support Agnes.

Agnes reached up with her arms and was happy to feel the strength of Flora and then Frank who pulled her out.

Poor Monty, whose legs felt awfully weak.

"I think I'm heavier than you, Monty." Beth was actually sure of it. She knew he was a lightweight, physically and emotionally.

Monty was now on Beth's shoulders. They looked like a circus act.

"Keep still, Beth."

"Monty, shut up. Put your arms in the air and do as the others did. You're such a liability sometimes."

"Piss off, Beth."

"Language, please!" requested Auntie Mildred. "This is no time for 'fucks' and 'pisses.'"

Did everyone just laugh?

Was anyone even taking this seriously?

Jordan certainly was. He knew what had happened now and how precarious their situation was. He needed to get himself and everyone else out of here.

Who knew where those murderers would be?

Standing up, he felt dizzy as hell, but he needed to be strong.

Beth climbed onto his shoulders. Given his height, it was so easy to pull Beth up.

Jordan assessed the situation.

He was going to have to use his gym skills to pull himself up.

He jumped and then fell.

Knowing that getting up there himself would be hopeless, he decided to do something else.

He returns to the door they had come through and kicks a plank of wood free.

Who knew how strong it would be? How long had it even been there?

Passing it through the hole, they rested it longways.

Gripping one end with his arms and the other with his feet, he somehow managed to get himself out.

Next, they were all sitting on the floor.

A moment of reflection.

"Jordan, I am so sorry." Auntie Mildred was just glad she hadn't killed him. For one moment, she thought she had and she rather liked him, so that would be a real shame. Now she knew he was alive, she took a moment to feel satisfied in knowing she was able to look after herself, almost like a ninja.

"Don't worry, Auntie Mildred, I'd have probably done the same to you." Auntie Mildred felt sickened by the thought of what could have been.

"Ladies and gents," Jordan's tone now very serious, "I cannot express how quickly we need to get back into the Gate House. Is it far, Frank?"

"Not really," replied Frank, who could honestly not remember how far it was. Too much had happened – it felt as though they'd been down here for hours.

Jordan replaced the lid and asked Frank to lead the way back.

No-one said a word.

No-one really took any notice of anything other than putting one foot in front of the other until they reached the hatch.

Above them, they could all see the light, the familiar smells and the warmth coming from the kitchen.

"You gotta love an AGA."

"I left it open in case we needed to flee and get back indoors in a hurry."

"Then let's all hurry!" Jordan was so thankful that there were steps. How easy that made things.

There were all of these new things to be grateful for. How their lives had changed in such a short space of time.

As soon as they were safely inside, Agnes glared at the floor.

"I have lived in this house for years. I've looked at that for years, covering it only because I thought it was a manhole cover.

The rug went back down.

"Is that locked?" Beth had concerns now.

"No. It doesn't lock," replied Jordan, understanding Beth's concerns.

"Then we need to take the rug off and expose the door. If they come up here, we need to be ready for them."

"I need to tell you all something and then I need to call the police."

CHAPTER FIFTEEN

"Did you hear that?"

There were now four men searching for the busybodies. They didn't really know how many of them there were.

As soon as they realised the door to the tunnel via the barn was locked, they knew they were inside.

These men were more familiar with the network of tunnels. They split into two and tried to flush them out from different directions.

They'd been walking for ages, hearing and seeing nothing.

Then suddenly, from their respective areas, they heard a bang. It was quite distinctive and seemed relatively close by. Both groups of two heard the same thing.

Independently of each other, both groups decided they would head towards where they thought the sound had come from.

Team A arrived first – they definitely heard movement above. It took them a little while to realise where the trapdoor was, but as soon as it was found, they had to work out how they would get through the hole.

Almost at the same time, Team B arrived. The four men stood beneath the opening.

"So, how're we getting up there?"

No-one really had the answer to that.

They sat on the floor, none of them worried about the dust. They looked at the opening once more.

"What's that there?"

"Dunno." One of them walked to the object on the floor and picked it up.

"It's that bloody old bat. That's the cosh she had in the horsebox."

Auntie Mildred would have corrected them, 'Those are Pretty Polly in sunblush and the ones in your hand are Pretty Polly in sherry'.

Know your nylons, boys!

"If she was down here, how on earth did she get back up?"

All four men suddenly seemed to have ignited determination. They were not about to be outwitted by an old woman.

With one man crouching down, another stood on top and hauled himself up. "Great pull up technique," the others remarked.

Another did the same, with less athletic style. The other two pulled up the third man, not at all slight. The crouching man was assisted by Jordan's plank of wood that the other men hadn't spotted.

"How far ahead do you think they are? It can't be more than 15 minutes?"

"Let's just go. Are you all prepared? This is going to be a messy one." That was certainly not a question.

In the safety and familiarity of the Gate House, Jordan stood and the others sat in the kitchen. Monty and Auntie Mildred had a glass of wine (actually, it was a mug of wine) and no-one else wanted anything to drink.

Flora had given Jordan some painkillers and put a cold compress on his head.

"I'd like you to go have that X-rayed as soon as, please, Jordan."

"Of course," said Beth.

"What do you have to tell us, Jordan?" Beth knew it had something to do with that room.

Jordan explained what he had found when he was fumbling around in the dark. Although he did say that he didn't feel a body, he described it as a shallow dent in the earth and had a rug over the top. He would put everything he had on it being a body.

Flora began to cry.

"How is this happening at our house? Who could it be, if it's anyone at all? This is terrible. I feel I should call my mother."

"Please, Flora, don't call anyone." Beth's turn now.

"Right now your mum is oblivious," hoped Beth, "and probably the rest of your family too, but we just don't know who is involved and you've seen all of that down there – these people know their way around. If you call your mum, you could be alerting these people and they could bugger off. Let's allow the police to do their job."

Jordan was on the phone to them at this point.

"OK," said Jordan coming off the phone. "They may be a little time. I've tried to explain everything and I have asked for urgent assistance. They were going to send a local plod, but I've said we need a team of people. I didn't really want to say there was a body because I didn't actually see one, but I did say there were people chasing us and we needed help, so hopefully they will be here soon."

"What if they come bursting through that trapdoor?" Beth supposed. "What if… has anyone even thought of this?… they come bursting through one of the actual doors? We are all huddled around here. We need to spread out around the house." Beth was thinking of all scenarios. The most obvious option isn't always the way it goes.

Agnes and Auntie Mildred were by the front door. They each had a knife. They actually felt quite safe; this was such a solid door without windows. Agnes checked the curtains were completely closed.

Flora stood by the patio door with a rolling pin in each hand. This door would be easier for anyone to break in through, but was also quite a solid structure.

Frank stood by the doorway between both rooms; this way, whichever door they came through, he would be there immediately.

Beth stood by the back door, also very robust, but it did have a small window in the middle, which she covered with a tea towel. She held a tenderizer in her hand.

Monty and Jordan sat beside the trapdoor.

All of the lights in the house were switched off.

The only element of light coming through the tea towel was

the outside light that was always on during the night. It provided enough illumination without being obvious.

Jordan had a frying pan and Monty, who had never really considered the need for kitchen tools and their use as weaponry, became flustered with the remaining choices, so instead, he picked up a syringe from the pile Flora had put on the worktop. He then took another, one for each hand.

"You know they are coming through here, don't you, Monty?"

Monty actually didn't know that. He'd rather hoped Auntie Mildred was their first line of defence – look how well she'd done with Jordan.

"I'm ready," he lied.

Without warning, a shot was fired.

The bullet splintered the surface of the trapdoor.

Jordan hadn't been expecting shots.

"Everyone upstairs. Lock yourselves in a room and do not come out! The police are on their way!" Monty shouted as loud as he could.

Now there was just Monty and Jordan in the kitchen.

Another shot was fired.

This time, it blew a hole right through the wooden door.

Jordan sat, heart pounding. They could only shoot upwards; he'd worked out the possible angles a bullet could come through.

They began to pound on the door. There were definitely a number of them.

Another shot.

Two arms appeared, a gun in one hand, a knife in the other.

Without any thought for his welfare, Monty surged forward and stabbed the arm holding the knife with his syringe.

Well, that had no effect.

The knife sliced through his trousers. Oh, the pain.

Why didn't the syringe do its job?

Realising he had left on the safety cap, he thought, *What a dickhead*!

Jordan, using his cricketing technique, batted both arms with his frying pan. The gun flew across the kitchen.

Monty ran to pick it up. This, he was sure, would be a useful thing to have, but hopefully it would never need to be used.

"Upstairs, Monty. Now!" demanded Jordan.

As soon as he knew Jordan was upstairs, he flew up behind him. They were all locked in the main bedroom.

The men could be heard forcing their way through.

"Where are the police?"

At that moment, there was a knock on the front door.

Hurrah! was the universal feeling.

It was the men who went to the door and opened it.

This wasn't right.

Something here is definitely not right.

The lock on the bedroom door was a good lock, but who knew if they had another gun?

They could hear voices.

"That sounds like my dad." Flora was suddenly pleased to hear her father's voice.

Running to the door to open it, Jordan stood in her way.

"No, Flora."

Stopping in her tracks, she looked straight at Jordan.

"What? But I'm sure it's my dad."

"Flora," Agnes began, putting her arms around her lovely friend, "your dad is obviously a part of all this somehow."

Flora dropped to the floor.

Then, a voice from the other side spoke out to them.

"If I were you, I would open this door now. We are armed and we have no issue shooting though this door, but we are coming in. Make no mistake about that."

It was indeed Lord Grey who was speaking.

"Dad!" shouted Flora. "What the hell..?"

"Flora, open the door!"

"I am not going to do that, Dad."

"Then you have shown your hand, Flora. You have given us no option."

"'Us'? Who is 'us'? I'm your daughter."

"I should think you are as unhappy about that as I am."

Flora was unsurprised by that statement.

"Then do what you have to, Lord Grey," was her response.

Agnes never believed a father to his daughter could say such hurtful words, but this comment cemented what she had always suspected about this hateful man.

She sent a text. No-one saw her do this.

"Stand back from the door and, Flora, if you try to stop me, it will be the last thing you do."

Everyone stood away from the door.

The gun blast was louder than before. Clearly a larger gun.

It didn't need a second shot; an arm came in and turned the key.

Monty was relieved he was standing behind the door when it was flung open.

Under normal circumstances, you could have laughed as his face stared through the hole blown by the shotgun.

Everyone noticed this and everyone thought the same thing, but this wasn't the time for laughter.

In walked Lord Grey and Felix, Flora's brother.

"Felix!"

"Oh, do shut up, Flora. You walk such a straight line. Agnes, oh dear Agnes, such a loyal friend, hanger-on; waiting for what, a handout? A free house, a new dress? What, Agnes, are you staying here for, you freeloader?"

"I stay because I love my job, Felix. I stay because I love your mother and sister. I stay because I love this house. All the things, Felix, both you and your father should love."

Lord Grey stared along the line-up.

"Who was there that night? Who saw the kid drop to the floor? We heard you."

And there it was, it had been Lord Grey in that room – but who was he with?

"It was me," Beth stood up, "I was alone."

"Oh no, my dear. You were *not* alone. We heard you talking to someone."

"She was talking to me on her mobile," Jordan stepped in.

All this time, Monty stood behind the door.

"So, who do I point this at, Flora? It can't be you. I feel nothing for you, but I can't kill you. Shall it be you, Old Lady? Or you, Agnes?"

"Do what you will, Lord Grey, and may you rot in hell for whatever it is you have done and are about to do."

The sirens were in, roaring. Several police cars and a van raced down the country lanes. Everyone in that room could hear them.

Two of the four men looked rather alarmed.

Lord Grey and his son seemed relatively nonplussed.

Lord Grey did not move; the gun was pointing directly at Auntie Mildred.

Louder they rang.

"Do you hear that, Guv?"

"Yes, I hear it. Probably the local plod. I can get rid of him. Don't worry."

Agnes knew this was not the local plod.

At their loudest, they stopped. Car doors banged. The noise outside would have been quite alarming had they not been involved in all this. It was certainly going to give the locals something to talk about for years.

"Open up! It's the police!"

Lord Grey handed the gun to Felix.

"I'll sort this," he said, making his way back downstairs and to the front door.

Felix stood holding the gun. The other two idiots were standing behind him; clearly they were the order takers rather than the givers.

"The first person to move will regret it!"

"You're not going to use that gun, Felix, no more than I am going to start doing the conga right now."

"Don't bank on that, Flora."

"Felix, what the heck are you doing? Why are you involved in this?" Agnes was still in a state of shock.

Lord Grey walked back up the stairs. "That got rid of them." He seemed convinced.

"What the hell..?" This seemed to be the universal phrase these days.

"So, people, what's it to be?" Lord Grey appeared to love this. He certainly seemed to have the whole thing planned out.

"Stop this, Dad."

Lord Grey laughed.

As he laughed, the front door opened. It wasn't forced; it was opened as a door should be opened.

They heard footsteps up the stairs and then Lady Grey walked into the room.

"How the hell did you get in?" Lord Grey was a little surprised to see his wife.

"Erm, I own the whole estate – remember?"

"I've brought a few friends with me. Come in, boys."

At least 10 police officers came up the stairs, at which point Lord Grey closed the door, back still turned against Monty.

"Everyone out of here, all except you, Old Lady."

He edged back and opened the door. The police stood on the other side. Given he was holding the gun and pointing it at Auntie Mildred, they were powerless right now.

Everyone filed out. Monty stood behind the door.

The police moved everyone down the stairs. Beth was looking for Monty, but couldn't find him.

She looked at Jordan. "Where's Monty?" she mouthed.

He pointed upstairs.

What does that mean?

"You know you will most probably die tonight, don't you, Old Lady?

"Well now, I'm nearer to 100 than I am 75, so I'd say if I'm going to go, I've had a good life. The thing is, I don't think I'm ready to go yet, so what happens now?"

Once again, Monty found some kind of inner strength, you know, the one he'd never found before. Well, here it was.

In his own ninja-like fashion (possibly the only thing other than his love of wine he had in common with his aunt), he pushed the door forwards and swiftly jumped on Lord Grey, pushing the syringe into Lord Grey's neck (safety cap off).

Lord Grey fell instantly to the floor; the gun did go off, but it was pointing towards the ceiling.

What a mess that made. At least it was a mess that could be fixed. No-one died. Auntie Mildred was still alive – he thought he saw her check herself over.

The police swarmed the room. Four officers took Lord Grey downstairs.

Monty ran to his aunt. They hugged. It was a real, meaningful hug. Neither wanted to let go of the other.

When they did, they walked downstairs. The rest of their friends ran towards them.

They all hugged one another.

Jordan was asked to go with the officers to the room where he had seen 'something'.

Beth, Monty and Auntie Mildred all had to give statements to the remaining officers.

Other officers comforted Flora, Agnes and Frank, but they too had to give statements.

CHAPTER SIXTEEN

Jordan entered the room with three officers; the amount of light was quite something.

He walked to the area where the rug lay.

"It's here."

The officers slowly peeled the rug away, revealing the body of a young man. Jordan had no idea who this was. He could see his hand was bandaged, but very bloody.

"He's missing a finger. That's in our freezer." Jordan explained what had happened with the fish guts.

Jordan was asked to leave the room when the officer wearing a special white suit came in.

He'd seen enough on various crime programmes to know what would happen next.

He was escorted back to the house.

He had to give a statement; both Beth and Monty were still providing theirs.

Following their statements, they were all asked to go into the kitchen where they were told what would happen next and also what they could and couldn't do.

This meant they could do nothing and couldn't do anything.

"Who was the person killed?" Flora needed to know.

"His name was Grant. He was the illegitimate son of Lord Grey." The officer could offer no more of an explanation.

Lady Grey, however, was able to fill in the gaps.

Agnes had called Lady Grey to ask for the murder squad to come to the Gate House.

Lady Grey had also made her way there.

Lady Grey felt the need to reveal she knew her husband had had an affair many years ago and had had several since. The most recent, however, he was about to leave her for.

Grant had decided it was time his dad took responsibility for his welfare. He had been in touch for some financial recognition.

Both Felix and his father were not prepared to see their 'share' of the financials being diluted for the sake of this outsider.

He meant nothing to Lord Grey.

He meant even less to Felix.

Everyone went home, not really knowing how to deal with this news.

Everyone literally wanted their own space to digest the past week or so.

Once inside their own home, Auntie Mildred said nothing. She grabbed a bottle of brandy and went upstairs. No glass.

Monty grabbed the ginger wine and also went upstairs – with a glass.

Jordan and Beth sat at the kitchen table.

"I need to go to sleep, Beth."

"Then let's go to bed." Beth was shattered.

Despite everything that had happened, everyone fell asleep immediately.

Flora, Agnes and Frank slept in the Hall that night.

"Talking is for the morning." Lady Grey knew the following day would be filled with questions. Tonight, of course, they all required their sleep.

Lady Grey had feelings of relief that she needed to understand before the morning.

Morning came for them all at different times.

Beth and Jordan sat in bed with a cup of tea. Neither of them really knew where to start.

"I love you, Beth."

"I love you too, more than you can ever know."

They had both closed their eyes, but sleep found neither of them; they were each trying to consolidate what had happened the night before.

Monty just sat up. He wasn't really thinking about anything. His mind was incapable of thinking. He found himself picking up his laptop and looking through the race card for the day. Surely he could find something that was running at any of the four courses and be able to associate with what had gone on over the last couple of weeks.

Auntie Mildred had slept. She thought she had woken up at one point, but didn't bother to engage her mind or her mouth. She concluded she was still asleep.

Beth's telephone rang. It was the police officer. They wanted to come over and speak to them all. They had a duty of care to make sure they were all OK.

Beth's phone rang again, this time it was Flora.

"Can we all come over this morning? The police are on their way and Mum has suggested they see us all together rather than having two meetings?"

"Of course, they have just called me too." Beth was halfway out of bed. "They said they'd be here around midday; why don't you get here just before?"

That was agreed.

Beth went downstairs. Made tea for everyone. As she handed it round, she told them about the police visit and the others coming round.

Everyone got ready; the house was silent.

Jordan decided to put on some relaxing music. He felt he needed it; surely the others did too.

Beth was going to take Jordan to the hospital to have his head checked out. Other than the massive headache that Flora had predicted, he felt OK. He assumed the adrenaline was still flowing through his veins and, as such, was acting as some kind of pain relief. Monty was going as well to see if he needed stitches in his leg from his wound. Flora thought not, but Monty was a little dramatic like that.

For shock, there was no treatment other than whiskey. Relief would take its time to find them all.

The others arrived first.

Lady Grey, Flora, Agnes and Frank. They walked into the kitchen. Beth was being mother and made fresh coffee (which seemed to be the most popular choice of beverage): strong and black, and for Auntie Mildred there was tea – and a wee dram.

Everyone confirmed they were OK under the circumstances, but they were all keen for the police to fill them in on what was actually happening now.

When the police arrived, there were six of them. Three were support officers. The others asked Jordan if he could go outside with them. Once outside, Jordan found a man dressed in white from top to bottom.

He'd come for the finger. Jordan removed it from the freezer in the garage, thankful they had put it in a freezer bag. At least it looked like they cared.

Back in the house, the police explained that Lord Grey and Felix had been charged with murder and perverting the course of justice. They couldn't really tell them any more at this stage. They explained they had been in touch with the boy's mother who was being comforted by the police.

"Apparently," began one officer, "Grant had been trying to have some kind of relationship with his father for years. It seems Lord Grey gave him the final brush-off. It was pure coincidence that there was a function at the Hall that night. He'd said he was going to make an announcement in front of everyone. Lord Grey knew that his wife could divorce him, leaving him with insufficient funds to maintain his lifestyle and Felix was not prepared to share his inheritance with another sibling so, in the heat of the moment, what happened, happened."

Lady Grey got to her feet.

"I am so sorry that you became involved in all of this. It is the saddest thing that has happened. You must all feel in complete shock, as do I, as do we all. I always knew there were tunnels beneath the grounds, but assumed they were all blocked off. They are hundreds of years old. The only thing that's ever been down there in the last 200 years is the Old Ghost."

"That's why Monty and I were there that evening. We were on

the ghost hunt, but no-one else was there. We thought they would be in the tunnels and then we found ourselves in that room."

"The ghost hunt was cancelled by me as it was double-booked with the function. So, that's your thing then, is it?" Lady Grey was looking at Monty and Beth mischievously.

"It is, yes; we love it."

"No, Beth – *you* love it, but need a plus one, which is me."

The police were writing much of the conversation down to build up a picture of that evening.

"Does anyone know who hit me that night?" Poor Auntie Mildred's assault had been ignored up to this point.

"Oh yes, Madam. Lord Grey and his son didn't work alone; they had two others with them doing the donkey work. They would have been responsible for the things that happened here to you. They are also in custody. I whacked him with *my* cosh."

Everyone laughed. Despite the whole situation, Auntie Mildred did what she does best; she brought a smile to everyone's face without even trying.

Almost three hours later, the police left.

Jordan had made bacon sandwiches for everyone. Flora had a couple of apples.

They talked for a while after the police had left. Lady Grey said they should all go to the pub for dinner one evening before Monty and Auntie Mildred returned to London.

The pair almost forgot they didn't actually live in the village.

"So, what now?" asked Frank.

"Let's get on with as normal a life as we can," offered Lady Grey.

The four of them stood up to go.

"I'll call you, Beth, when I've booked a table."

As they left, Beth caught Flora taking Frank's hand. Agnes turned and smiled back at Beth.

Auntie Mildred felt quite happy that she would see Burt again. Maybe she'd have her last hurrah with him that night.

"What now, Monty? What's our next adventure going to be?"

"Beth, when I go home, I never want to see you ever again. I will delete your number from my phone. In fact, once I've left, I'm deleting you from my life."

Beth laughed out loud.

"Yeah right, Monty. You know you love me. You also know I'll be calling you and you'll pick up."

Monty smiled at that.

Of course he knew that.

Auntie Mildred also smiled.

Somehow, she knew she would be involved in their next adventure.

WHO'S WHO

Beth Evans-Silverton

The wife of Jordan – lucky enough not to have to work. Spends her time reading about haunted properties anywhere in the UK – keen to drag Jordan and her best friend, Monty, with her to check out ghoulish sightings. Her favourite reading materials are murder mystery books and oftentimes her fictional literature is confused with reality.

Jordan Evans-Silverton

The husband of Beth, he runs a very successful business mining silver. His mine is in Australia so is often away, but when home, enjoys the company of his wife and the stories she tells of the spectres she reads about. He isn't quite so keen on racing around the darkness of the countryside to scare himself half to death, but secretly does enjoy the unexpectedness of it all.

Monty Peebles

Best friend of Beth, they have known each other for 15 years. Their worlds should never have collided – Monty is of vague royal descent and they met when Beth almost choked on a drink in a London bar. Monty (she claims) saved her life. He enjoys each and every ghostly journey they pursue. As a writer, he takes notes of their experiences, writing in his notebook for future reference. Monty is extremely well-read and a complete literary genius. Quite how they have remained such good friends when they had such little in common when they met is a mystery in itself – Beth puts this down to him being her saviour and that they will be friends forever. Monty feels duty bound to make sure nothing untoward happens to Beth whom he knows firsthand to be more accident-prone than anyone he has ever met before in his life. He also knows she is the most adventurous of his friends.

Lady Grey

The sole heir to the estate. Only child to a mother who longed for a second child. This was, however, thwarted by the DNA results of an illegitimate child whose mother had been encouraged with a hefty cheque to disappear, along with her child. So ended her mother's longing for a sibling.

Lady Grey used to be a loving wife, which was lost on her arrogant husband. Her world, now that her children are less dependent on her, is the estate and its upkeep. Lady Grey loves this house; its size is not remotely intimidating, it's the only house she has ever lived in. She has no desire to leave and enjoys entertaining guests and telling the stories that have been passed down to her (mostly historical infidelities and the resident ghost – a story that attracts a lot of interest with the National Ghost Hunters). This provides a distraction from her rather dull life and even more mundane marriage – not her choosing – she is convinced her husband is having an affair, but has yet to substantiate this. She has been trying to reignite their relationship unsuccessfully for years, now settling for 'this is it, then'.

Lord Grey

Marrying into the family, Lord Grey believes he is as entitled as his wife to the wealth and trappings of her estate. As the man of the house (not that this was his ancestral home) he believes his word is the only word. Lord Grey is a pompous toad. Not everyone likes him, including both the children (although their son knows how to work him to his advantage). He likes his wife, but no longer loves her; he is unable to leave since that would restrict his lifestyle and the importance he places upon himself would clearly wane.

Master Felix Grey

The elder of the two children. Spoilt, arrogant, heir in waiting. Rude, self-indulgent, collector of anything he can lift of any real worth (usually acquired at the dinner parties of neighbouring estates, the hosts usually too preoccupied to notice they had been removed let alone by whom). At 26, he has never worked a day in his life – what would be the need? He has all the money he could ever wish to waste.

Lady Flora Grey

At 24, a lovely girl. Kind, gentle and very hard-working. Lady Flora works as a nurse at the local hospital where no-one has any idea of her lineage. Lady Flora hates her father and has nothing in common with her brother other than their parents. Flora does, however, love her mother more than anyone else. Nevertheless, her confidant is Agnes who has been the housekeeper since before she was born.

Agnes (the housekeeper)

Poor old Agnes. Following the death of her husband, Agnes has lived alone in the Gate House on the estate. Prior to his death, her husband had worked as the head gardener on the estate, primarily protecting trees from the increasing numbers of deer. Agnes loves the Gate House, it is homely and welcoming and the family has encouraged her to invite friends to stay. Agnes has never had children but loves them, for she is very close to Lady Flora (who she calls Flo). Agnes is the only person whom Flora can speak to, knowing whatever she has to say would go no further. Agnes takes great pride in her appearance, often visiting the vintage shop in the village where she was once fortunate enough to pick up a couple of designer dresses that she was sure had once belonged to Lady Grey.

Frank (the gardener/handyman)

Over the years, Frank (born Franklyn – a name he chooses never to use), has worked his way up from general lad to taking over from Agnes' husband. A very quiet young man, now at 22 he has found his place – a decent wage and accommodation in the Gate House with Agnes (she does bake a lovely steak pie). Frank has a real fondness for Flora – he will sit with both ladies listening to their chatter until such a point he knows to leave – as directed by Agnes, indicating Flora has something on her mind she wishes to share with her friend and confidant. Once, Frank had to go to A&E – he had slipped on some wet leaves and twisted his ankle. That was when he first knew Flora was working there. He remembers her complete professionalism – she hardly acknowledged him.

Burt (the landlord of the public house in the village)

Ruddy complexion to go with his ruddy awful manner. Burt will become less offensive as the wine flows. Ironically as the landlord, he sits on the wrong side of the bar. His consumption of alcohol must wipe off any balance sheet profits. That said, as much as he drinks, he doesn't miss a trick – anything that goes on in the village Burt knows about it. The hotter the gossip the better his mood. As a singleton, he is always looking for love; the chances of that happening reduce on a daily basis (oh, and he wears shirts that don't tuck in properly so he has a belly that hangs out the front and a rather disgusting bottom view when he turns around).

Auntie Mildred (the Old Maid Aunt of Monty Peebles).

Rather demanding and unpopular with almost everyone she meets.
Oh Auntie Mildred, what a character. Mid-80s, never married,

but has opinions on marriage, husbands, wives, how to treat each other, children, grandchildren, infidelity, loyalty, including how to keep a man and how to lose one. Auntie Mildred loves Monty, but there is little visual evidence of this. Auntie Mildred swears like a trooper, drinks like a fish, dislikes people in general and rides a moped when living in her home in London. Auntie Mildred had previously only met Beth only on one occasion, which happened to be in the bar when Beth almost choked to death on her drink. Auntie Mildred thought this highly amusing – who chokes on liquid? Lightweight! The unusual thing about Auntie Mildred – whilst she dislikes almost everyone apart from Monty, but she does in fact like Beth – is that they have spoken several times over the years. Auntie Mildred spends a lot of time in Africa where she runs a business. A remarkable lady for her age, she puts this down to good food and even better wine.

Printed in Great Britain
by Amazon